John Young Sargent

Easy Passages for Translation Into Latin

John Young Sargent

Easy Passages for Translation Into Latin

ISBN/EAN: 9783337388461

Printed in Europe, USA, Canada, Australia, Japan

Cover: Foto ©Andreas Hilbeck / pixelio.de

More available books at **www.hansebooks.com**

Clarendon Press Series

EASY PASSAGES

FOR

TRANSLATION INTO LATIN

BY

JOHN YOUNG SARGENT, M.A.

Fellow and Tutor of Hertford College, Oxford

SEVENTH EDITION

Oxford

AT THE CLARENDON PRESS

M DCCC LXXXIX

PREFACE TO THE SEVENTH EDITION.

A great many new passages have been substituted for old ones in the present edition, and this has made a rearrangement necessary. In addition to the pieces set in Pass Examinations in the Oxford Schools, others set in the Class Schools, in College Scholarships, and various Competitive Examinations have been admitted.

Owing to this extension some of the new exercises will be found harder than the generality of those which appeared in previous editions. It seemed, however, that a sufficient number of easy passages had been retained to warrant the retention of the old title. These will be found chiefly at the beginning, and are calculated to lead up to the more difficult ones that follow. The references to Latin authors will be found useful in helping the student to deal with the latter by suggesting an appropriate style and syntax.

Also more examples of continuous narrative have been inserted; partly to engage the interest of the learner, and partly to give the teacher an early opportunity, as similar expressions recur, of judging how far his hints and instructions have been appreciated.

J. Y. SARGENT.

NOTICE.

A Key to this Edition of Sargent's Easy Passages for Translation into Latin has been prepared, and will be supplied to Teachers only, on application to the Secretary to the Delegates, Clarendon Press, Oxford.

Post free, price 5s.

CONTENTS.

A.

viii CONTENTS.

CONTENTS.

Y.

PASSAGES

FOR

TRANSLATION INTO LATIN.

1. The Dorian army marched to Athens, and lay
encamped under its walls. Aletes, their leader, had
previously consulted the Delphic oracle, and had been
assured of success, provided he spared the life of the
Athenian king. A friendly Delphian, named Cleomantis,
disclosed the answer of the oracle to the Athenians, and
Codrus resolved to devote himself for his country/ He
went out at the gate, disguised in a woodman's garb, and
falling in with two Dorians killed one with his bill, and
was killed by the other. The Athenians now sent a
herald to claim the body of their king, and the Dorian
chiefs, deeming the war hopeless, withdrew their forces
from Attica.

2. So now in the hour of danger the geese heard the
sound of the enemy, and they began to cry in their fear
and to flap their wings; and Marcus Manlius, whose
house was in the Capitol hard by the temple, was
aroused by them; and he sprang up and seized sword
and shield, and called to his comrades, and ran to the
edge of the cliff. And behold a Gaul had just reached
the summit, when Marcus rushed upon him and dashed

B

his shield into his face and tumbled him down the rock. The Gaul as he fell bore down those who were mounting behind him ; and the rest were dismayed, and dropped their arms to cling more closely to the rock, and so the Romans, who had been roused by the call of Marcus, slaughtered them easily, and the Capitol was saved.

Livy, v. 47.

3. Jupiter himself appeared to a citizen in a dream, and bade him tell the consuls not to lay down their office without being reconciled. On this Pompeius stood still, and said not a word ; but Crassus advanced, took his hand, and exclaimed, 'My countrymen, I am doing nothing ignoble or mean in being the first to give way to Pompeius, whom you deemed worthy of the name of Magnus before he had a beard, and twice decreed him a triumph before he was a senator.' Such was the ceremony which Pompeius demanded of his equals ; to the multitude he was still more haughty. He withdrew himself from the business of an advocate, on which the most illustrious citizens had been wont to pride themselves ; and he never went into the forum unless surrounded by a company of nobles.

4. Julius Atticus, the father of Herodes, must have ended his life in poverty had he not discovered an immense treasure buried under an old house, the last remains of his patrimony. According to law the emperor might have asserted his claim to the treasure trove. But when Atticus gave voluntary information of his good luck, the equitable Nerva who then filled the throne, refused to accept any part of it, and commanded him to

use without scruple the present of fortune. The cautious Athenian still insisted that the treasure was too large for a subject, and that he knew not how to use it. 'Abuse it then,' replied the monarch, with good-natured peevishness, 'for it is your own.'

5. Day at last dawned, but did not quite clear up the mystery of the night's alarm to the mass of the inhabitants of Tarentum. They were safe in their houses, unmassacred, unplundered; the only blast of war had been blown by a Roman trumpet; yet Roman soldiers were lying dead; and Gauls were spoiling their bodies. Suspense at length was ended by the voice of the public crier summoning the citizens of Tarentum, in Hannibal's name, to appear without their arms in the market-place; and by repeated shouts of 'Liberty! Liberty!' uttered by some of their own countrymen who ran round the town calling the Carthaginians their deliverers. The firm partizans of Rome made haste to escape into the citadel, while the multitude crowded to the market-place.

6. They found the market-place regularly occupied by Carthaginian troops; and the great general, of whom they had heard so much, was preparing to address them. He spoke to them, in Greek apparently, declaring, as usual, that he was come to free the inhabitants of Italy from the dominion of Rome. 'The Tarentines, therefore, had nothing to fear, they should go home, and write each over his door, *a Tarentine's house*; those words would be a sufficient security, no door so marked should be violated. But the mark must not be set

falsely upon any Roman's quarters; a Tarentine guilty
of such treason would be put to death as an enemy; for
all Roman property was the lawful prize of the soldiers.'
Accordingly all houses where Romans had been quartered were given up to be plundered, and the Carthaginian soldiers gained a harvest, says Polybius, which
fully answered their hopes.

7. Upon receiving this answer, the Adelantado burnt
several villages, and approached nearer to the camp of
Maiobanes. Fresh negotiations were entered into : Maiobanes convoked an assembly of his people, and they
contended that Geryones ought to be given up, and
cursed the day when first he came amongst them. Their
noble chief, however, said, 'that Geryones was a good
man, and deserved well at his hands, for he had given
him many royal gifts when he came to him, and had
taught him and his wife to join in choral songs, and to
dance, of which he made no little account; wherefore he
would not desert Geryones, since he had fled to him,
and he had pledged himself to protect the fugitive; and
would rather suffer all extremities than give detractors a
cause for speaking ill, to say that he had delivered up
his guest.'

8. Now when the Delphians heard what danger they
were in, great fear fell on them. In their terror they
consulted the oracle concerning the holy treasures, and
inquired if they should bury them in the ground, or
carry them away to some other country. The god, in
reply, bade them leave the treasures untouched. 'He

was 'able,' he said, 'without help to protect his own.' So the Delphians, when they received this answer, began to think about saving themselves. And first of all they sent their women and children across the gulf into Achæā. After which the greater number of them climbed up into the tops of Parnassus, and placed their goods for safety in the Corycian cave ; while some effected their escape to Amphissa in Locris. In this way all the Delphians quitted the city, except sixty men and the prophet.

9. The son of Crœsus, although old enough to talk, was unable to speak, and even afterwards, when nearly grown up, could not utter a word, but was for a long time thought to be dumb. But when his father had been defeated in battle, and the city where he dwelt taken, and a soldier with a drawn sword was going to slay him not knowing that he was the king, the young man opened his mouth and tried to speak, and in the effort burst the impediment which made him tongue-tied, and spoke out plainly and articulately, crying to the man 'not to kill Crœsus the king.' Then the soldier lowered his sword, and the king's life was spared, and from that time forth the youth had the use of his voice.

10. A party had been sent to Saxona to get bread ; for the inhabitants of that island had always been friendly to the Spaniards, and were in the habit of supplying them with provisions. The Cacique of the place, with a stick in his hand, was urging his men, and hastening the preparations. The Spaniards were looking on : one of them had his dog with him, and the animal was wild to get at the Cacique. The Spaniard could hardly hold it in ; and unfortunately happened to say to a comrade standing by him, 'what a thing it would be if he were to set the dog at him.' His friend, in jest, said, 'At him,' thinking that the Spaniard could certainly restrain the dog. But with this encouragement it burst from its master, rushed on the Cacique, and killed him in a manner hideous to behold.

Livy, xxix. 42, 43.

11. Alcibiades, the Athenian, was brought up as a boy at the house of his uncle Pericles, where he was instructed in the liberal arts and accomplishments. Pericles also ordered Antigenides the flute-player to be sent for, to give him lessons in flute-playing, which was then considered a very genteel thing. When the flute was handed to Alcibiades, he put his mouth to it, and blew ; but was so ashamed at the distortion of his face, that he immediately dashed down the flute, and broke it. The occurrence became generally known and talked about, and the result was, that by common consent flute-playing ceased to be fashionable among the Athenians.

12. While the King lay in his blood, a noise and tumult arose in the town, and Tanaquil ordered the gates of the royal house to be shut, to keep out the people. And she spoke to them out of an upper window, and said that the king was not dead, but only wounded, and had ordered that Servius should reign in his stead until he had recovered. Therefore Servius filled the king's place, and sat as judge on the royal throne, conducting all affairs as the king himself was wont to do.

But when it became known, after some days, that Tar-
quinius had died, Servius did not resign the royal power,
but continued to rule for a time, without being appointed
by the people and without the consent of the Senate.
Then, after he had won over a large number of the
people by all kinds of promises and by grants of land,
he held an assembly and persuaded the people to choose
him for their king.

Livy, i. 41.

13. The Prefect set out, accompanied by seventy horsemen and three hundred foot-soldiers. Anacaona, who had
probably some suspicion of his intentions, summoned all
her feudatories around her, to do honour to him when
she heard of his coming. Then she went out to meet
him with a concourse of her subjects. Various amusements were provided for the strangers, and Anacaona
thought that she had succeeded in propitiating this severe
looking Governor, as she had done the last. / But the
former followers of Roldan were about the Governor,
telling him that there was certainly an insurrection at
hand, and that if he did not look to it now and suppress
it at once, the revolt would be far more difficult to quell
when it did break out.

Livy, i. 9.

14. Ovando listened to these men, indeed he must
have been much inclined to believe them, and professed
himself convinced that an insurrection was intended.
With these thoughts in his mind, he ordered that on a
certain day, after dinner, all the cavalry should get to
horse, on the pretext of a tournament. The infantry
too he caused to be ready for action. He himself, a

Tiberius in dissembling, went to play at quoits, and was disturbed by his men coming to him, and begging him to look on at their sports.   The poor Indian queen hurried with the utmost simplicity into the snare prepared for her.   She told the Governor that her Caciques, too, would like to see the tournament.

Livy, i. 9.

15. Upon this Ovando, with demonstrations of pleasure, bade her come with all her Caciques to his quarters, for he wanted to talk to them, intimating, as I conjecture, that he would explain the show to them.   Meanwhile he gave his cavalry orders to surround the building; he placed the infantry at certain commanding positions, and told his men that when in talking with the Caciques he should place his hand upon the badge of knighthood which hung upon his breast, they should rush in and bind the Caciques and Anacaona.   It fell out as he had planned.   All these deluded Indian chiefs and their Queen were secured.   She alone was led out of Ovando's quarters, which were then set fire to, and all the chiefs burnt alive.   Anacaona was afterwards hanged, and the province was desolated.

Livy, i. 9.

16. After the overthrow of Critias, Pausanias, king of the Lacedæmonians, came to the assistance of the Athenians.   He made a peace between Thrasybulus and those who were in possession of the city, on the following conditions : 'that no one, except the thirty tyrants, and the ten magistrates who succeeded them and had emulated their cruelty, should be condemned to banishment, or have their property confiscated, and that the

control of state affairs should be restored to the people.'
The following circumstance too redounds to the credit
of Thrasybulus, that after the reconciliation had been
made, being now possessed of great influence in the
state, he carried a law, 'that no one should be accused
or punished for acts done previously to the peace.' This
law they called an amnesty. He was not content, however, with merely passing the law; he found means to
carry it into execution. For when one of the companions of his exile wished to take the lives of those
with whom a reconciliation had been made, he issued a
public prohibition, and performed what he had promised.

17. There was then an illustrious Roman, Appius
Claudius by name, who, on account of his great age and
the loss of his sight, had ceased to attend the Senate.
But when he heard of the embassy from Pyrrhus,
and the report prevailed that the Senate was going to
vote for the peace, he could not contain himself, but
ordered his servants to carry him in his chair through
the forum to the Senate-house. When he was brought
to the door, his sons and his sons-in-law received him
and led him into the Senate. A respectful silence was
observed by the whole body on his appearance, and he
delivered his sentiments in the following terms :—
'Hitherto I have regarded my blindness as a misfortune, but now, Romans, I wish I had been as deaf as
I am blind : for then I should not have heard of counsels
so ruinous to the glory of Rome.' No sooner had he
finished speaking than the Senate voted unanimously
for the war.

Cicero, *de Senectute*, §§ 16, 17.

18. After the battle of Panormus, the hopes of the Romans rose again, and the Senate gave orders to build a third fleet of two hundred sail. But the Carthaginians, weary of the war, thought that a fair opportunity of making peace was now offered : and that the Romans had not so entirely recovered from their late disasters, but that they would gladly listen to equitable terms. Accordingly an embassy was despatched to offer an exchange of prisoners, and to propose terms on which a peace might be concluded. Regulus (according to the well-known story) accompanied this embassy, under promise to return to Carthage if the purposes of the embassy should fail. On his arrival at Rome, he refused to enter the walls, and take his place in the Senate, as being no longer a citizen or a senator. Then the Senate sent certain of their own body to confer with him in presence of the ambassadors, and the counsel which he gave confirmed the wavering minds of the fathers.

19. Antiochus in the pride of his heart was showing Hannibal the vast forces he had got together to make war upon the Romans, and was pointing out his regiments resplendent with silver and gold ornaments, and showing the scythed chariots, the elephants with their towers, and the horsemen in all their bravery with shining bits and saddles and trappings/ Filled with vain-glory by the contemplation of such a vast and well-appointed host, he looked at Hannibal and said, 'Well, do you think that will do? Do you think all that will be enough for the Romans?' The Carthaginian, with a covert allusion to the cowardice of those soldiers in their costly armour, replied, 'Enough? O yes, all that will certainly be enough for the Romans, be they ever so greedy.' Nothing could be more courteous, and at the same time more cutting, than this answer. The king was thinking of his army as a match for the Romans; Hannibal, as so much booty.

20. Sedition was spreading among the tribes of that region, when Camillus advanced with his forces to repress it by a sudden blow. The defence of the peaceful province had been entrusted to one legion with a few bands of the allies; and this little army was enough to overcome all resistance in the field. Tacfarinas, relying on the arts which he had learnt from his late masters, ventured to give battle, and suffered a speedy defeat. The pro-consul claimed the honours of a conqueror; and Tiberius, it was believed, was more willing to grant them on account of the obscurity of his name, which had shone with no splendour since the old days of the Gallic invasion. Camillus himself had had no experience in arms; nor was he now elated by success, or tempted to think himself a mighty general. He was not indeed aware how short his triumph would be.

21. Although serving in the ranks he had more influence than his superiors; and the soldiers gave more heed to him than to their officers. This circumstance hastened his death. For he bade his pilot steer into the harbour in his eagerness to be the first to enter, and this cost him his life. For he got in, indeed, but the others did not follow. And so he was surrounded by a swarm of enemies. While bravely fighting, his vessel was struck, and began to sink. He might have escaped by throwing himself into the sea, because the allied fleet was close at hand, and ready to take on board all in danger of drowning; but he resolved to die rather than desert his ship. The rest were not so scrupulous, but swam to shore. But he, holding that an honourable death is preferable to a disgraced life, was slain as he fought hand to hand with the enemy.

22. Then replied that valiant knight, sir Marmaduke, 'Surely, my friends, it shall never be said of me, that I drowned myself for nothing. Do not ye so either, but follow me, and I will clear a passage through them even to the bridge.' Then spurring his charger, he plunged among the enemy, and dealing blows on either side passed unhurt through the throng, and laid open a wide path for his followers. For he was tall and stout of body. And as he fought thus valiantly, his nephew, who was wounded, his horse being slain, shouted after him, 'Sir, save me!' He replied, 'get up behind me.'— 'I cannot,' he answered, 'for my strength is gone.' Presently, his comrade, an esquire of the same sir Marmaduke, came up, and descending from his horse, he placed the young man on it, and said to his master, 'Sir, go where you will, I follow.' And he followed him to the bridge, so that both were preserved. All who remained, to the number of a hundred horsemen and five thousand foot, perished, except a few who swam the river.

Livy, ii. 10.

23. In a moment the fortune of the day was changed, and the pursuers in their turn took to flight. Many were killed in the shock of the encounter, and many as they

endeavoured to escape. And they not only perished
by the sword, but rushing blindly into the swamps many
were swallowed up, horses and all, in the bottomless
mud. The king himself was in great danger; for his
horse being wounded fell and threw his rider headlong
to the ground, so that he narrowly escaped being killed
where he lay. ¹ He was saved by the devotion of a
knight, who hastily dismounted, and lifted the trembling
king into his own saddle. The knight, being unable on
foot to keep up with the retreating horsemen, was overtaken by some of the enemy who had hurried up on
seeing the king fall, and by them stabbed to death.
The king having skirted the marsh, succeeded in reaching
his camp, where most of his followers had given him up
for lost.

24. We are told that Valerian, in chains, but invested
with the imperial purple, was exposed to the multitude, a
constant spectacle of fallen greatness, and that whenever
the Persian monarch mounted on horseback, he placed
his foot on the neck of a Roman emperor. Notwithstanding all the remonstrances of his allies, who repeat-
edly advised him to remember the vicissitude of fortune,
to dread the returning power of Rome, and to make his
illustrious captive the pledge of peace not the object of
insult, Sapor still remained inflexible. When Valerian
sank under the weight of shame and grief, his skin,
stuffed with straw and formed into the likeness of a
human figure, was preserved for ages in the most celebrated temple of Persia, a more real monument of
triumph than the fancied trophies of brass and marble
so often erected by Roman vanity. The tale is moral

and pathetic, but the truth of it may fairly be called in question.

25. The next year the Portuguese mariners discovered the island of Madeira. But in their first attempt to cultivate the land they met with an untoward accident. In clearing the forest they kindled a fire which spread and burnt for seven years, and in the end the timber which had given the island its name became its rarest commodity. But Cape Bojador on the African coast long formed the limit of discovery in a southern direction. This cape was formidable in itself, being terminated by a ridge of rocks with fierce currents running round them, but was much more formidable from the fancies which mariners had formed of the sea and land beyond it. 'It is clear,' they were wont to say, 'that beyond this cape there is no people whatever : the land is as bare as Libya—no water, no trees, no grass in it : the sea so shallow that at a league from the land it is only a fathom deep; the currents so violent that the ship which passes that cape will never return.'

26. When Dolabella was proconsul of Asia, a woman of Smyrna was brought before him. This woman had taken the lives of her husband and son, by secretly administering a draught of poison. Moreover, she confessed the crime, and said that she had good reasons for doing it, because the said husband and son had laid wait for and murdered another son of hers by a former husband, an excellent young man who had done them no harm. That the facts were so there was no dispute. Dolabella put the case before his council. But none of the judges ventured to deliver sentence in so doubtful a case; since on the one hand the crime of poisoning had been admitted, and ought not, they thought, to go unpunished; while on the other hand, a well-deserved punishment had been inflicted on two malefactors. Dolabella referred the matter to the court of Areopagus at Athens. The Areopagites, having heard the case, bound over the accuser and the accused to come up for judgment that day one hundred years.

27. One of the ringleaders was a certain Michael Joseph, a blacksmith, a notable talking fellow, and no less desirous to be talked of. The other was Thomas Flammock, a lawyer, who by telling his neighbours commonly upon any occasion that the law was on their side had gotten great sway amongst them. This man talked learnedly, and as if he could tell how to make a rebellion, and never break the peace. He told the people that subsidies were not to be granted or levied in this case : that is, for wars in Scotland, for that the law had provided another way of raising means for these journeys ; much less when all was quiet, and war was made but a pretence to poll and pill people. And therefore that it was good they should not stand now like sheep before the shearers, but put on harness, and take weapons in their hands.

Livy, xxii. 25, 26.

28. Very just and neat is the reproof administered to Albinius by Cato. Albinius composed a history of Rome in Greek. In the beginning of the book he writes to the following effect: that no one has a right to be hard upon him if there occur any passages wanting in correctness or

elegance. ' For,' he says, ' I am a native Roman, born in Latium ; Greek is quite a foreign language to me.' And on that ground he asked pardon and forgiveness for any mistakes there might be. When Cato had read it, he exclaimed, ' Nay then, friend Aulus, you are surely trifling with us, since you have chosen rather to beg forgiveness for a fault, than to avoid committing the fault. For we are wont to ask forgiveness, either when we have erred unwittingly, or sinned under compulsion. But as for you, who, pray, compelled you to commit a fault, for which you had to ask forgiveness before committing it ? '

29. Darius in the letter which he sent to Alexander assumed a tone of remonstrance, as one who had suffered an unprovoked aggression. He reminded Alexander that his father had been on terms of peace and alliance with Ochus, but on the accession of Arses had commenced hostilities, without any just cause, against Persia ; and that since he himself had mounted the throne, Alexander instead of sending an embassy to renew the ancient amicable relations between the two kingdoms, had invaded his territories, and forced him to wage war in self-defence. He was now reduced by the chance of war to make a request ; such, however, as one king might becomingly address to another : that Alexander would restore his mother, wife, and children. He himself was willing to become Alexander's friend and ally, and desired that he would send ministers with the two Persian envoys to treat with him.

30. On the road some Persian scouts fell into his hands, from whom he learnt that Darius, with an army far greater than he had before brought into the field, lay on the left bank of the Tigris, prepared to guard the passage against him. He now advanced at full speed towards the Tigris ; but when he reached it, found neither Darius himself nor any hostile force, and met with no other obstacle in the crossing than the rapidity of the stream. On the left bank he gave his troops a few days' rest after their forced march, during which there occurred an eclipse of the moon. Aristander expounded it as a sign that during that month the Persian monarchy was destined to lose its power and glory ; and when Alexander sacrificed to the moon, the sun, and the earth, as the powers which concurred to produce the portent, the victims were found to announce a victory.

31. The cruelty wreaked by the Spaniards upon their captives was excessive. Las Casas mentions that on one occasion they hanged up thirteen Indians 'in honour of Christ and His twelve Apostles.' These men hanging at such a height that their feet could just touch the ground, were used as dumb figures for the Spaniards to try their swords upon. On another occasion he saw some Indians being burnt alive in a sort of wooden cradle. Their cries disturbed the Spanish captain, taking his siesta in his tent, and he bade the alguazil, who had charge of the execution, to despatch the captives. This officer, however, only gagged the poor wretches, who thus fulfilled their martyrdom in the way he originally intended for them.

Livy, xxix. 42, 43.

32. The young prince, trained in a school of deceit, maintained the character of his race for cunning. With tears he implored the general not to send him away: not even a royal crown was so dear to him, he said, as the sight of Cortes. Cortes, not unmoved himself, checked the boy's tears, and saying, that if such were his feelings he would soon have him back again, sent him away to his own people. But like a tiger let out of prison, finding himself free, he began to carry on the war against his benefactor with such vehemence, that the tears he shed at the interview would seem to have been tears of joy. Many of the Spanish officers, friends of Cortes, were glad that this had happened, and that his excessive forbearance had been mocked by the young traitor; as if Cortes had been influenced solely by good nature, and not by motives of the deepest policy.

33. The messengers who were sent to entrap these simple islanders, said that they were sent by God to convey the Lucayans to the islands of the blest, where dwelt their ancestors, and the dear ones they had loved when alive. Under this pretext great numbers were decoyed from their home and carried away to Hispaniola, to work the rest of their days in the mines. When they learnt the truth, some refusing sustenance perished by hunger, some lived on in patient despair, and some endeavoured to escape and return to their native land. One Lucayan, who had been a carpenter in his own island, having made his way through the woods to the northern coast, cut down a tree, and having laid the stems of smaller trees across beams made of the main trunk, lashed them together with the stringy roots of certain shrubs which grow there, and filling in the interstices with leaves and twigs, thus constructed a kind of raft.

34. He then laid in a store of maize, and some vessels of water as provisions for the voyage. He took on board with him another Indian man and a woman, all three being related to each other. Having provided themselves with paddles they set out, with the north star for their guide. For many days and many nights they rowed and drifted; Hispaniola, their loathed prison, had long been out of view; they had already gone two hundred miles, and were already hoping to see Lucaya once more. 'Cheer up, sister,' says the Indian, 'not many mornings more will dawn upon us before we behold our native land again.' When lo, a dark object is seen on the skyline. At first they rejoice, thinking their native land is in sight. Soon, however, their joy is turned into despair. That which they thought to be land is a Spanish caravel. It has already seen the raft, and bears down swiftly upon the fugitives. They are seized and carried back to Hispaniola.

35. The countess, fearful of the fate that awaited her children if they were taken, declared that she would rather kill them with her own hand than let them fall into the tyrant's power. But her husband recoiled with horror at the dreadful suggestion, and said that he would put them under the protection of some friends abroad, and would himself escort them on their journey. Accordingly they set out for Venice, to attend the annual festival on St. Mark's day. After spending the day there

C 2

at the religious celebration, they embarked about one
o'clock in the morning, when every one was sound
asleep, on board a vessel prepared for the purpose, as
if to return home, but their real destination was Corfu.

36. But the wind was contrary, and morning overtook
them while still but a short distance from the land. The
royalists who garrisoned the port sent an armed cruiser
to seize their vessel and bring it back, with stringent
orders not to return without it. As they drew near, the
count applied himself to encouraging the rowers, from
time to time raising his hands to heaven and praying to
God for help. But this high-spirited lady nerved herself
to carry out the resolution she had long before taken.
She mixed a draught of poison, and produced a sword.
Then having placed the bowl before her, and unsheathed
the sword, she said, ' Death is our only refuge ; there lie
the roads to death; choose each his own way, and
escape the tyrant's cruelty. Come, sirs, the eldest first,
take the sword, or drain the cup if you prefer the slower
death.' Their enemies were close upon them ; the
countess was urgent. Then some chose the poison, and
some the sword, and dying threw themselves from the
ship. The brave lady and her husband, clasped in the
embrace of death, leapt overboard, and sank beneath the
waves. The king's men captured an empty vessel.

37. They had been informed that Sir Marmaduke
Langdale (whom they still called their general), after the
overthrow of the Scottish army, had been taken prisoner,
and remained in Nottingham castle under a most strict
custody. Morrice, with a party of twelve horse, a choice

band, sallied forth in the beginning of the night, with a resolution to take Rainsborough prisoner, and thereby to ransom their general. They were all well acquainted with the country and knew the ways exactly, and went so far, that about daybreak they put themselves into the common road that led from York. The guard, expecting no enemy in this direction, negligently asked them ' whence they came ? ' and they negligently answered : and asked again, ' where their general was ? ' saying, ' they had a letter for him from Cromwell.'

38. The guards sent one to show them where the general was, which they knew well enough, and that he lay at the best inn of the town. And when the gate of the inn was opened to them, three of them entered, the rest rode on to the other end of the town, to the bridge over which they were to pass towards Pomfret. Here they expected and did find a guard of horse and foot, with whom they entertained themselves in discourse, saying, ' that they stayed for their officer, who only went in to speak to the general,' and called for some drink. The guards, making no question of them being friends, sent for drink, and talked negligently with them of news ; and, it being now broad day, some of the horse alighted, and the foot went to the court of guard, conceiving the morning's work to be over.

39. They who went into the inn, where nobody was awake but the fellow who opened the gate, asked in which chamber the general (for so all the soldiers called Rainsborough) lay ; and the fellow showing them from below the chamber door, two of them went up, and the other stayed below, and held the horses, and talked with the soldier who had walked with them from the guard. The two who went up opened the chamber door, found Rainsborough in his bed, but awaked with the little noise they had made. They told him in short 'that he was their prisoner, and that it was in his power to choose whether he would be presently killed' (for which work he saw they were very well prepared), 'or quietly, without making resistance, to put on his clothes, and be mounted upon a horse, that was ready below for him, and accompany them to Pomfret.'

40. The present danger awakened him out of the amazement he was in, so that he told them he would wait upon them, and make the haste that was necessary to put on his clothes. One of them took his sword, and so they led him downstairs. He that held the horses had sent the soldier away to those who were gone before, to bid them get some drink, and anything else that could be made ready, against they came. When Rainsborough came into the street, which he expected to find full of horse, and saw only one man, who held the others' horses, and presently mounted that he might be bound behind him, he began to struggle and cry out. Whereupon, when they saw no hope of carrying him away, they immediately ran him through with their swords, and leaving him dead upon the ground, they got upon their horses, and rode towards their fellows, before any in the inn could be ready to follow them.

41. When those at the bridge saw their companions coming, which was their sign, being well prepared, and knowing what they were to do, they turned upon the guard and killed so many of them, that the rest fled in distraction, so that the way was clear and free; and though they missed carrying home the prize, for which they had made so lusty an adventure, they joined together, and marched, with the expedition that was necessary, a shorter way than they had come, to their garrison; leaving the town and soldiers behind in such a consternation, that, not being able to receive any information from their general, whom they found dead upon the ground, without anybody in view, they thought the devil had been there; and could not recollect themselves which way they were to pursue an enemy they had not seen.

42. Rhodes, an island of ancient renown, with its capital, a rich fair city of the same name, was being beleaguered by Demetrius, a general of great repute in his day, who from his skill and experience in conducting sieges, and his knowledge of the engines employed in the taking of towns, had gained the name of Poliorcetes. In the course of the siege, a certain house belonging to the municipality, standing outside the walls, was marked out for attack, and he was preparing to dismantle it, and then burn it to the ground. Now in this house was kept the famous portrait of Ialysus, the handiwork of Protogenes, an illustrious painter; and Demetrius was jealous enough to grudge the Rhodians the possession of this masterpiece.

43. The Rhodians sent envoys to Demetrius with this message: 'What possible reason can you have for wanting to destroy that picture by burning yonder house down? For if you overcome us all, and capture the entire town, you will, through your victory, become owner of the picture untouched and unharmed ; but if you fail to vanquish us, and raise the siege, we bid you reflect, whether it is not a mean thing because you cannot conquer the Rhodians in war, to make war upon Protogenes now dead.' When he had heard these words of the envoys, he raised the siege, and spared both the picture and the city.

44. The place, like the hill-forts of India, was an isolated rock, precipitous on all sides, and only accessible by a single narrow path. Provisions had been laid in sufficient, it was thought, even if the siege should last for two years. Alexander himself, when he saw it, was almost inclined to despair. But he sent Cophas to summon Arimazes to surrender. The chief received the message with derision, and asked whether the Macedonians had wings. In no other way did it seem possible for an enemy to reach the summit. The taunt roused Alexander to a resolution which he would allow no obstacle to foil. He proclaimed a reward of ten talents for the man who should first mount to the top, and a sum proportionately less for each of the next nine. The lowest prize was to amount to three hundred darics. The most agile and expert climbers in the army. soon came forward as competitors for wealth and honour, to be earned by a risk which they were used to despise.

Sallust, Bell. Jugurth. 92 sqq.

45. They provided themselves with cords and with a number of iron pegs with which the tents were secured, and set out in the middle of the night toward the most precipitous, and consequently the most neglected side of the rock. The attempt would perhaps have been utterly desperate, if the ascent had not been rendered easier by the snow which lay on the ground, and which had become so solidly frozen, that the pegs when driven into it could support the weight of the body. Still, more than thirty of the adventurers lost their footing, and were buried so deep in the snow at the foot of the hill that their bodies could not afterwards be found. Their more fortunate companions, who gained the summit in safety, announced their success to their friends below by the waving of flags, the signal which Alexander had appointed. As soon as he saw it he again sent Cophas to summon Arimazes, and to point out to him that the Macedonians had found wings.

Sallust, *Bell. Jugurth.* 92 sqq.

46. Of our hero's moderation and wisdom many examples might be given. We will content ourselves with one, from which it may be easily inferred how popular he was with his countrymen. When a young man he had occasion to plead his own cause at Athens, and not only acquaintances and personal friends came to support him, but Jason the tyrant also, the most powerful potentate of the day, attended. Jason, although at home in his own country he dared not go abroad without a bodyguard, came to Athens without any escort, and paid his friend Timotheus the high compliment of risking his own life in order to be present, rather than fail to support Timotheus when defending his honour. At a later day he conducted the war against Jason, by command of

the people : deeming the claims of country more sacred than those of private friendship.

47. But the Rhegine general, Phyton, was detained with all his kindred, and reserved for a different fate. First, his son was drowned by order of Dionysius ; next Phyton himself was chained to one of the loftiest siege-machines, as a spectacle to the whole army. While he was thus exhibited to scorn, a messenger was sent to apprise him that Dionysius had just caused his son to be drowned. 'He is more fortunate than his father by one day,' was the reply of Phyton. After a certain time the sufferer was taken down from this pillory, and led round the city, with attendants scourging and insulting him at every step, while a herald proclaimed aloud, 'Behold the man who persuaded the Rhegines to go to war, thus signally punished by Dionysius!'

48. Milo of Crotona, the famous athlete, came to a strange and miserable end. Being now advanced in years, he had given up his profession, and happened to be travelling alone in a woodland district of Italy, when he saw an oak tree by the wayside, with spreading branches, but hollow in the centre. Wishing (I suppose) to try whether he still retained aught of his former strength, he thrust his fingers into the hollow of the tree, and endeavoured to rend the trunk asunder. And he succeeded in splitting the timber, and pulling apart the sides. But as soon as Milo relaxed his hands, think-ing the task was accomplished, the oak returned to its natural position, when the pressure was removed, and, closing tightly over the poor fellow's hands, held him there a prisoner, until he was devoured by wild beasts.

49. Travelling through a forest with a marsh on each side of the road, he recollected some reason for going back, and ordered the driver to turn. He did not do so instantly, and Paul repeated the order. 'In a moment,' the man replied, 'here the road is too narrow.' Paul flew into a passion, jumped out of the carriage, and called to an equerry to stop the driver and chastise him. The equerry endeavoured to allay the storm by assurances that the carriage would turn as soon as possible. 'You are a scoundrel as well as he,' was the reply ; 'he shall turn even though he break my neck : at all hazards he shall do as I bid, the moment I give the order.' Meanwhile the coachman had done so, but too late to save himself from a sound beating.

50. An order against wearing boots with coloured tops was rigorously enforced. By the Czar's order the police officers stopped a gentleman driving through the streets in a pair. He remonstrated, and said he had no others with him, and certainly would not cut off the tops of those : upon which the officers seizing each a leg as he sat in his droschky, pulled them off, and left him to go barefoot home.

Coming down a street the emperor saw a nobleman who had stopped to look at some workmen planting trees by his order. 'What are you doing?' said he. 'Merely seeing the men work,' replied the nobleman. 'Oh ! is that your employment? Take off his pelisse, and give him a spade. There now—work yourself !'

51. One pathetic yet ludicrous occurrence is mentioned in connexion with the practice of suicide among the Indians. A number of them belonging to one master had resolved to hang themselves, and so to escape from their labours and their sufferings. The master being made aware of their intention, came upon them just as they were about to carry it into effect. 'Go seek me a rope too,' he exclaimed, 'for I must hang myself with you.' He then gave them to understand that he could not live without them, as they were so useful to him; and that he must go where they were going. They, believing that they would not get rid of him even in a future state of existence, agreed to remain where they were; and with sorrow laid aside their ropes to resume their labours.

52. The following anecdote is related of Sertorius :— A white hind, of remarkable beauty and extreme swiftness, had been given to him as a present by a certain Lusitanian. Sertorius set about to make people believe that this creature had come into his possession supernaturally; that it was inspired by Diana, and that it held conversations with him, warning and instructing him what was best to do. And if it happened that any disagreeable duty had to be imposed on his soldiers, he used to give out that he had been advised by the hind. When he had said that, all obeyed willingly as if obeying God. One day an alarm was raised of a sudden attack by the enemy. The hind, frightened by the bustle and tumult that followed, ran away and hid in a neighbouring marsh : and afterwards, search having been made in vain, was supposed to have perished.

53. Not many days after, news was brought to Sertorius that the white doe was found. Thereupon he bade the messenger be silent, and tell no one under pain of punishment. At the same time he gave him instructions, to loose the doe next day and let her suddenly come into the room where he should be with a company of his friends. When his friends had arrived the following day, Sertorius told them that he had dreamt that the lost doe had come back to him : and, as she had been wont, advised him what he ought to do. He then gave a signal, the doe was let loose, and came running into the chamber of Sertorius. Cries of astonishment and admiration arose. The credulity of the barbarians was of great use to Sertorius in important matters. It is recorded that out of all the tribes which made common cause with Sertorius, although he suffered many defeats, not a man ever deserted from his side, although savages as a rule are fickle in their allegiance.

54. The Pharos is a tower of great height and marvellous construction, built on an island, from which it takes its name. This island by its position forms a breakwater and harbour for Alexandria. A pier has been run out to the length of nine hundred feet, the work of early kings, and connects it with the town by means of a narrow causeway and a bridge. There are many dwelling-houses on the island, and a village as big as a town. The people are wreckers, and are accustomed to plunder all ships that by want of skill or stress of weather are driven out of their course in this direction. The Pharos commands the entrance to the harbour, which is so narrow that no ship can enter if the occupants of the tower wish to prevent it.

55. I never was more astonished in my life than when I halted on the top of one of the numerous hills of which this portion of the Crimea is composed, and looking down saw under my feet a little pond closely compressed by the sides of high rocky mountains. On it floated six or seven English ships, for which exit seemed quite hopeless. The bay is like a Highland tarn, and it is long ere the eye admits that it is some half-mile in length from the sea, and varies from two hundred and fifty to one hundred and twenty yards in breadth. The shores are so steep and precipitous that they shut out, as it were, the expanse of the harbour, and make it appear smaller than it really is. Towards the sea the cliffs close up, and completely overlap the narrow channel which leads to the haven, so that it is quite invisible. On the south-east of the poor village, which struggles for existence between the base of the rocky hills and the margin of the sea, there are the extensive ruins of a fort, built some two hundred feet above the level of the sea.

56. In ancient records the following story is told about the Sibylline books. Once upon a time, an old woman, a stranger, came to the court of Tarquin the Proud, bringing with her nine books, which she asserted were inspired oracles, and said she wanted to sell them. Tarquin asked the price. The woman named an extravagant sum. The king laughed at her for an old crazy woman. Thereupon she walked to the fireplace, took three of the books, and burnt them before his face. She then asked the king whether he would buy the remaining six at the same price. At this the king laughed louder than ever, 'This old crone,' he said to himself, 'is undoubtedly mad.'

57. Thereupon the woman burnt three more volumes on the spot, and then calmly repeated her demand that he would give her the same price for the remaining three. At length Tarquin's interest was aroused; his face grew serious; he began to think that such persistence was not without a motive, and ought not to be treated lightly. And so he purchases the three remaining books at the price originally asked for the nine.

The woman then went her ways; and was never more seen upon earth. The three books were stored away in one of the temples; and the priests have recourse to them as oracles whenever it is necessary to enquire the will of Heaven.

58. One day, it was the eighth of August, very early in the morning, by reason of the heat the mariners began to bring-to their vessels, and, as they had been commanded, to draw forth those captives from the hold. Whom, placed together on that plain, it was a marvellous sight to behold, for amongst them there were some of a reasonable degree of whiteness, handsome, and well made; others less white, resembling leopards in their colour; others as black as Ethiopians, and so ill-formed, as well in their faces as their bodies, that it seemed to the beholders as if they saw the forms of a lower hemisphere. But no heart, how hard soever, but was pierced with sorrow, seeing that company; for some had sunken cheeks and their faces bathed in tears, looking at each other; some were groaning very dolorously, with eyes fixed upon the heavens, crying out loudly as if they were asking for succour from the Father of nature; while others struck their faces with their hands, and threw themselves on the earth.

59. But now for the increase of their grief came thos¢
who had the charge of the distribution, and they begar
to put them apart one from the other, in order to equalis¢
the portions; wherefore it was necessary to separate
children and parents, husbands and wives, and brethrer
from each other. Neither in the partition of friends anc
relations was any law kept, only each fell where the lo
took him. So the partition was not made without grea
difficulty; for while they were placing in one part th¢
children that saw their parents in another, the childrer
sprang up perseveringly and fled to them ; the mother;
enclosed the children in their arms and threw themselve;
with them on the ground, receiving wounds with littl¢
pity for their own flesh, so that their offspring might no
be torn from them. And besides the trouble they hac
with the captives, the plain was full of people from th¢
neighbourhood, who in that day gave rest to their hands
the mainstay of their livelihood, only to see this novelty.

60. The admiral set sail at sunset, favoured by a ligh
breeze from the south. About midnight, however, th¢
wind fell, and drifting with the current they were drivei
out of their course, so that when day broke they saw th¢
Cuban coast left far away to larboard. But taking ad
vantage of the turn of the tide, they made all speed b
rowing to reach that part of the island, where from th
experience of the last summer they knew a landing coul¢
best be effected. And here the zeal of the men wa
especially commendable, who by unremitting labour a
the oar enabled the transports and tenders to keep u
with the galleys of war. All the ships reached land b
noon. No enemy was in sight at that point. A larg

body had assembled there, but frightened by the number of the approaching ships, had withdrawn from the coast, and retired further up the country.

61. Notwithstanding the almost insuperable difficulties of such a navigation, he persisted in his course with his usual patience and firmness, but made so little way, that he was three months without seeing land. At length his provisions began to fail; the crew was reduced to the scanty allowance of six ounces of bread a day to each person. The admiral fared no better than the meanest sailor. But, even in this extreme distress, he retained the humanity which distinguishes his character, and refused to comply with the earnest solicitations of his crew, some of whom proposed to feed upon the Indian prisoners which they were carrying over, and others insisted on throwing them overboard in order to lessen the consumption of their small stock. He represented that they were human beings reduced by a common calamity to the same condition with themselves, and entitled to share an equal fate. His authority and remonstrances dissipated those wild ideas suggested by despair. Nor had they time to recur, as he came soon within sight of the coast of Spain, and all their fears and sufferings ended.

62. With the theft of the Palladium may be compared the exploit of Fernando Perez del Pulgar at the siege of Granada. 'Who will stand by me,' said he, 'in an enterprise of desperate peril?' The Christian cavaliers well knew the rash hardihood of del Pulgar, yet no one who heard hesitated to step forward. He chose fifteen companions, all men of powerful arm and dauntless heart. In the dead of night he led them forth from the camp, and approached the city cautiously, until he arrived at a postern gate which opened upon the Darro, and was guarded by foot-soldiers. The guards, little thinking of such an unwonted attack, were for the most part fast asleep. The gate was forced, and a confused and chance-medley skirmish ensued.

63. Fernando stopped not to take part in the fray. Putting spurs to his horse he galloped furiously through the streets, striking fire out of the stones at every bound. Arrived at the principal mosque, he sprang from his horse, and kneeling at the portal took possession of the edifice as a Christian chapel, dedicating it to the Blessed Virgin. In testimony of the ceremony, he took a tablet which he had brought with him, on which was inscribed in large letters, Ave Maria, and nailed it to the door of the mosque with his dagger. This done, he remounted his steed, and galloped back to the gate. The alarm had been given, the city was in an uproar ; soldiers were gathering from every direction. They were astonished at seeing a Christian warrior speeding from the interior of the city. Fernando, overturning some, and cutting down others, .rejoined his companions, who still maintained possession of the gate by dint of hard fighting, and they all made good their retreat to the camp.

64. Having waited for a south wind they set sail, and on the second day ran past Avlona and Durazzo. They were descried from the mainland, and Captain Coponi, then in command of the fleet at Durazzo, immediately put to sea, and the wind falling, had nearly come up with our squadron, when it began to blow a gale from the south, which proved our salvation. He did not, however, give up the chase, hoping by perseverance and good seamanship to weather the storm, and as the frigates drove before the gale in a northerly direction, none the less continued the pursuit. Our fellows, while making the most of their good luck, were in mortal dread of being captured, in case the wind should fall. Finding a haven, called Lady's Bay, three miles beyond Lissa, they ran their vessels in there—this haven is protected from the south-west but not safe from the south—thinking less about danger from the weather than from the enemies' fleet. However, as soon as they had got into port, by miraculous good fortune the wind, which had been blowing forty-eight hours from the south, chopped round to the south-west.

65. This change of wind completely turned the tables. Those who had lately been in a fright, found themselves ensconced in a snug haven ; and those who had been threatening destruction to our ships began to fear for their own. The tempest in fact protected our men, but so shattered the Turkish fleet that every one of their decked ships, sixteen all told, were dashed to pieces and destroyed, and out of their immense multitude of sailors and marines part were battered to death on the rocks, part hauled ashore by our men : all these latter were saved and sent home by our admiral.

Two of our vessels, being slower sailers, were overtaken by night, and not knowing where the rest had taken refuge, anchored right opposite Lissa. These

Osman Bey, in command at Lissa, prepared to capture, sending out a number of pinnaces and small craft for the purpose, but at the same time offered to treat for their surrender, and promised quarter to those who should give themselves up.

66. One of these two vessels had on board 220 men drafted from a levy of recruits, the other less than 200, but all seasoned hands. And now one may see what advantage there is in courage and constancy. The raw hands, frightened by the number of the vessels, and brought low by the tossing and sea-sickness, accepted the enemies' assurance that they would do them no harm, and surrendered themselves to Osman. They were all brought before him, and in violation of his solemn oath, put to death most cruelly before his eyes. But the veterans, who had been exposed no less to the beating of the storm, and the sickening smell of the bilge-water, never dreamt of flinching or showing the white feather. But having got through the first part of the night in haggling about terms, on pretence of surrendering, they compelled the sailing master to run the ship ashore. Then, having found a defensible position, they passed the rest of the night there, and when Osman sent a troop of horsemen to capture them, they made a brave defence, and after killing not a few of their opponents made their way in safety to the head-quarters of our army.

67. The bedchamber was in an upper story, accessible only by a removable staircase or ladder, at the foot of which there lay every night a fierce mastiff chained, and a Thracian soldier tattooed after the fashion of his

country. The whole house moreover was regularly occupied by a company of guards; and it is even said that
the wardrobe and closets of Thebe were searched every
evening for concealed weapons. These numerous pre-
cautions of mistrust however were baffled by her artifice.
She concealed her brothers during all the day in a safe
adjacent hiding-place. At night Alexander, coming to
bed intoxicated, soon fell fast asleep, upon which Thebe
stole out of the room—directed the dog to be removed
from the foot of the stairs, under pretence that the
despot wished to enjoy undisturbed repose—and then
called her armed brothers.

68. After spreading wool upon the stairs in order that
their tread might be noiseless, she went again up into
the bedroom, and brought away the sword of Alexander,
which always hung near him. Notwithstanding this encouragement, the three young men, still trembling at the
magnitude of the risk, hesitated to mount the stairs; nor
could they be prevailed upon to do so, except by her
distinct threat, that if they flinched, she would awaken
Alexander and expose them. At length they mounted,
and entered the bedchamber, where a lamp was burning;
while Thebe, having opened the door for them, again
closed it, and posted herself to hold the bar. The
brothers then approached the bed; one seized the
sleeping despot by the feet, another by the hair of the
head, and the third with a sword cut his throat.

Cicero, *de Off.* ii. 7.

69. As soon as Philippus had left the meeting and gone
home, and betaken himself to rest in an upper chamber,

Xenoclides delivered the fortified posts of the town to the charge of certain of the conspirators, surrounded the palace with a guard, and stationed sentinels at the doors, with orders not to leave them. He then caused a galley to be manned and armed, and put it under the command of his brother, instructing him to keep moving up and down the harbour as if to exercise the rowers, thinking that if fortune baffled their plans, he would have a means of retreat left. He then selects from among his followers certain young Byzantine nobles, of great personal strength and courage. These he commissioned to go to Philippus, without their arms, as if they merely came to see him. They were admitted on being recognized.

70. As soon as they got inside they barred the door, and fell upon Philippus as he lay in bed, and proceeded to bind him. A great noise and uproar ensued loud enough to be heard outside. And here one may observe how unpopular irresponsible monarchy is, and how miserable the life of an autocrat who desires to be feared rather than loved. For his body guards, if they had been well disposed to him, might have broken the doors open and saved the emperor's life, while the conspirators who were unarmed, were calling aloud for a sword to those outside as they held their victim alive. No one however interfered to save him; but one Seuthes, a Thracian, handed them a sword through the window, and with this Philippus was despatched.

71. Don Pedro was the legitimate heir to the throne of Castille. Henry and Fadrique were his half-brothers, children of Leonora de Guzman. When Pedro succeeded to the throne, at his mother's instigation he put her rival to death. His brothers Henry and Fadrique escaped, and the former renounced his allegiance ; the latter fled into Portugal, but after some time he made his peace, returned, and was appointed master of the order of St. Iago. When several months had elapsed, he was invited to join the court at Seville, and take his share in the amusements of an approaching tournament. He accepted the invitation, but was sternly and ominously received, and immediately executed within the palace. The friends of Pedro asserted that the king had that very day detected Fadrique in a correspondence with his brother Henry and the Arragonese, while popular belief attributed the slaughter of the Master to the influence of Pedro's mistress Maria de Padilla.

72. The natives however were not deficient in strategy. Their commanders ordered proclamation to be made all along the line, that no one should leave his post, that the booty was theirs, and whatever the foreigners left would fall into their hands ; they must make up their minds to conquer, as everything depended on that. The antagonists were fairly matched in numbers and in courage. Our men it is true had been deserted both by fortune and by their leader, yet they had confidence in their own prowess, and whenever one of our squadrons made a charge, great numbers of the enemy fell. Seeing this, the barbarian chief gave orders to his men to fight at long range, and not to come to close quarters, and to fall back whenever the English made a charge, (they were lightly armed, and their agility from constant training was so great that they could do this without loss,) and to press on in pursuit whenever the English retired.

73. Favorinus once administered the following rebuke to a young pedant whose affectation it was to use antique and obsolete words in ordinary conversation. 'Curius and Fabricius and Coruncanius,' said he, 'in their day, and the three Horatian brothers in times still more remote talked plainly and intelligibly to their contemporaries, and used not the language of the Auruncans or the Sicanians or the Pelasgians, the original inhabitants of Italy, but that in vogue in their own day; but you, as if you were talking with Evander's grandmother, must needs employ words gone out of use ages ago. I suppose the fact is you don't want to be understood. If so, hadn't you better be silent altogether? But perhaps it is the innocence, the integrity, the modesty, the sobriety of the ancients that you emulate. In that case I would say, let your conduct be old fashioned, your conversation modern.'

74. If the gods thought that I had wronged them they would not have omitted to punish me when they caught me in the greatest danger. For what danger can be greater than a sea-voyage in winter-time? The gods had then both my life and my property in their power, and yet they preserved me. Was it not then open to them so to manage, as that I should not even obtain interment for my body? Have the gods then preserved me from the dangers of sea and pirates merely to let me perish at Athens by the act of my villainous accuser Cephisius? No, sirs, the dangers of accusation and trial are human, but the dangers encountered at sea are divine. If therefore we are to surmise about the sentiments of the gods, I think they will be extremely displeased and angry if they see a man, whom they themselves have preserved destroyed by others.

75. He then went on to warn the members of the league that they ought to form their estimate of friends by their deeds, and not by their words, and should ascertain who were to be trusted and who were not. ' Use your freedom sparingly,' he said. ' Liberty, when kept well in hand, is a serviceable thing both for individuals and for states : when pushed to excess it becomes a source of danger to others, and is apt to run away with and prove fatal to its possessors. Let the various classes within each state, high and low, and no less the several states among themselves, do their best to promote concord. For as long as you are united neither king nor potentate will be strong enough to crush you. Discord and sedition offer continual opportunities to the adversary, for the faction that is worsted in domestic conflicts, is more fain to throw itself into the arms of the foreigner, than to submit to a fellow-citizen.'

76. These soldiers, all Greeks and mercenaries, fighting for a country not their own, encountered each other on the field of battle like enemies—but conversed in a pacific and amicable way, during intervals, in their respective camps. Both were now engaged, without disturbing each other, in catching eels amidst the marshy and watery ground between Epipolæ and the Anapus. Interchanging remarks freely, they were admiring the splendour and magnitude of Syracuse with its great maritime convenience—when one of Timoleon's soldiers observed to the opposite party—'And this magnificent

city, you, Greeks as you are, are striving to barbarize,
planting these Carthaginian cut-throats nearer to us than
they are now; though our first anxiety ought to be, to
keep them as far off as possible from Greece.'

77. Fortune suddenly changed sides.   When Antony
returned to Italy, everyone thought that Atticus would
be in great danger, on account of his intimacy with
Cicero and Brutus.   And so on the arrival of the
generals he had withdrawn from public, fearing proscrip-
tion.   He lay concealed at the house of P. Volumnius,
to whom, as we said above, he had rendered assistance :
(for so continual in those days were the vicissitudes of
fortune that now these now those found themselves at
the summit of success or in the depth of adversity ;) and
had with him Gellius Canius, a man of his own age and
not unlike him in character.   Atticus' goodness of heart
is proved by the fact that he lived on such close terms
with Gellius, whom he had known as a boy at school,
that their friendship went on increasing to the end of
their lives.

78. We went downstairs directly, highly contented to
have found such a protector.   The street was covered
with the dead and dying ; their cries were enough to
have pierced the hearts of the most savage barbarians.
We walked over the bodies, and when we arrived at the
church of St. Catharine, met an officer of distinction on
horseback.   This generous person soon discovered us,
and seeing me covered with blood, said to the person
who conducted us, 'Fellow soldier, take care what you
do to these persons.'   At the same time he said to my

wife, ' Madam, is yonder house yours ? ' My wife having answered that it was, ' Well,' added he, ' take hold of my stirrup, conduct me thither, and you shall have quarter.' Then turning to me, and making a sign to the soldiers with his hand, he said to me, ' Gentlemen of Magdeburg, you yourselves are the occasion of this destruction, you might have acted otherwise.'

Pliny, Epist. vi. 16 ; vi. 20.

79. The soldier who had used me ill, took this opportunity to steal away. Upon entering my house we found it filled with a multitude of plunderers, whom the officer, who was a colonel, ordered away. He then said he would take up his lodging with us, and having posted two soldiers for a guard to us, left us with a promise to return forthwith. We gave with great cheerfulness a good breakfast to our sentinels, who complimented us on the lucky fortune of falling into their colonel's hands ; at the same time, representing to us that their fellow soldiers made a considerable booty while they continued inactive merely as a safeguard to us, and therefore beseeching us to render them an equivalent to a certain degree.

80. Upon this, I gave them four rose-nobles, with which they were well contented, and showed so much humanity as to make us an offer to go and search for any acquaintance whom we desired to place in safety with us. I told them I had one particular friend, who had escaped to the cathedral, as I conjectured, and promised them a good gratuity on his part if they saved his life. One of them, accompanied by my maid servant,

went to the church, and called my friend often by name ;
but it was all in vain, no one answered, and we never
heard mention of him from that time.

Pliny, *Epist.* vi. 16 ; vi. 20.

81. But the spirit of the French army was now exhausted ; they had laboured and fought without inter-
mission for fifty days, they had spared neither fire nor
sword, and Zaragossa was still unconquered. ' Before
this siege,' they exclaimed, ' was it ever heard that twenty
thousand men should besiege fifty thousand ? ' Scarcely
a fourth of the town was won and they themselves were
already exhausted. ' We must wait,' they said, ' for re-
inforcements, or we shall all perish among these cursed
ruins, which will become our own tombs before we can
force the last of these fanatics from the last of their dens.'
Marshal Lasnes, unshaken by their murmurs, and obstinate to conquer, endeavoured to raise the soldiers'
hopes. He pointed out to them that the losses of the
besieged so far exceeded their own, that the Spaniards'
strength must soon be wasted, and their courage must
sink, and that the fierceness of their defence was already
abated ; but if, contrary to expectation, they should renew the example of Numantia, their utter destruction
must quickly ensue from the combined effects of battle,
misery, and pestilence.

Livy, xxi. 20.

82. The Samnites, attacked at once by two consular
armies, were compelled to divide their forces ; and eight
thousand men were detached from the army before Aquilonia to relieve Cominium. A deserter acquainted Papirius

with this movement; and he instantly sent off a messenger to warn his colleague, while he himself attacked the enemy at the moment when he knew their force to be thus untimely weakened. The auspices had been reported to be most favourable; the fowls ate so eagerly, so said their keeper to the consul, that some of the corn dropped from their mouths on the ground. This was the best possible omen. But just as the consul was on the point of giving the signal for action, his nephew, Sp. Papirius, came to tell him that the keeper had made a false report.

Livy, x. 40; Cicero, de Divinat. ii. 34.

83. 'Some of his comrades have declared the truth,' said the young man: 'and far from eating eagerly, the fowls would not touch their food at all.' 'Thou hast done thy duty, nephew, in telling me this,' replied his uncle; 'but let the keeper see to it if he has belied the gods. His report to me is that the omens are most favourable, and therefore I forthwith give the signal for battle. But do you see,' he added to some centurions who stood by, 'that this keeper and his comrade be set in the front ranks of the legions.' Ere the battle-cry was raised on either side, a chance javelin struck the guilty keeper, and he fell dead. His fate was instantly reported to the consul. 'The gods,' he exclaimed, 'are amongst us: their vengeance has fallen on the guilty.' When he spake, a crow was heard just in front of him to utter a full and loud cry. 'Never did the gods more manifestly declare their presence and favour,' exclaimed the consul; and forthwith the signal was given, and the Roman battle-cry arose loud and joyful.

Livy, x. 40.

84. The Samnites met their enemies bravely; but the awful rites under which they had been pledged, gave them a gloomy rather than a cheerful courage : they were more in the mood to die than to conquer. On the Roman side, the consul's blunt humour, which he had inherited from his father, spread confidence all around him. In the heat of battle, when other generals would have earnestly vowed to build a temple to the god whose aid they sought, if he would grant them victory, Papirius called aloud to Jupiter the victorious, 'Ah, Jupiter, if the enemy are beaten I vow to offer to thee a cup of honeyed wine, before I taste myself a drop of wine plain.'

Livy, x. 41, 42.

85. Such irreverent jests do not necessarily imply a scoffing spirit : they mark superstition or fanaticism as much as unbelief; nor would the consul's language shock those who heard it, but rather assure them that he spoke in the full confidence of being heard with favour by the gods, as a man in hours of festivity would smile at the familiarity of an indulged servant. Besides, Papirius performed well the part of a general : he is said to have practised the trick which was so successful at Bannock-burn : the camp servants were mounted on baggage mules, and appeared in the midst of the action on the flank and rear of the Samnites; the news ran through both armies that Sp. Carvilius was come up to aid his colleague, and a general charge of the Roman cavalry and infantry at this moment broke the Samnite lines and turned them to flight. The mass of the routed army fled either to their camp or within the walls of Aquilonia; but the cavalry, containing all the chiefs and the nobility of the nation, got clear from the press of fugitives, and escaped to Borranum.

Livy, x. 40.

86. The faithless foe only sought an opportunity for treachery. They allowed a few days to pass by, and then when our soldiers were slack and off their guard, made a sudden sally from the gates, choosing the hour of noon, when some were absent and some were taking their siesta without leaving the entrenchment, wearied with their incessant labour. The enemy took advantage of a high wind to set fire to the works. The wind caused the flames to spread so rapidly that the rampart, the curtain, the tower, and the artillery caught fire at once and were consumed before any knew how the disaster had happened. Our men in sudden alarm snatched up any weapons that came first, hurried out of the camp, and dashed upon the enemy. But they were prevented by a cloud of arrows and missiles from the wall from following up the pursuit.

87. The Greeks resolved to return to the camp, and arrived there at the hour of supper, which they greatly needed, as when they began the battle they had not yet made the morning meal. But they found that the camp had been plundered of their whole stock of provisions, and were almost all forced to pass the night fasting. The next morning they learnt the death of Cyrus from two messengers sent to them by Ariaeus, who announced that he would wait for them until the next day, but should then set out on his return to Ionia. Clearchus, in the name of the other generals, bade them carry word

back to Ariaeus that the Greeks were victorious and undisputed masters of the field, and that it had been their intention to march against the king: and they now offered to place Ariaeus on the throne. The messengers were accompanied by Cheirisophus and Meno, who, having been a guest and friend of Ariaeus, was desirous of being employed on the mission.

88. In the meanwhile, to provide themselves with a meal, the Greeks were compelled to slaughter their beasts of burden, and to dress their food with the arrows, shields, and other relics of the battle, which they found at a short distance from the camp. Toward noon some Persian heralds came from the king, accompanied by Phalynus, a Zacynthian, who had gained credit with Tissaphernes by his pretensions to military skill. They were commissioned to summon the Greeks to lay down their arms, and throw themselves upon the king's mercy. Just as they had delivered their message, Clearchus happened to be called away to inspect a sacrifice: and having merely remarked, that it was not usual for conquerors to surrender their arms, he desired his colleagues to return such an answer to the proposal as might appear to them most becoming. Cleanor, an Arcadian, who was the eldest among them, then declared that they would die sooner than give up their arms.

89. It was already evening, and they had not yet so much as settled on a safe place in which to bestow their prisoner for the night. At last some one suggested the treasury, an underground dungeon walled and vaulted with stone. Into this the prisoner was let down, the aperture closed with a large stone worked by machinery. The next day the more moderate part of the population, remembering his former services to the state, proposed that he should be pardoned, and employed in procuring some alleviation of their present ills. The rebel leaders, however, who were now in power, after secret consultation resolved unanimously to put him to death. The only question was whether the sentence should be carried out immediately. The more bloodthirsty party carried the day; and a messenger was sent with a draught of poison. He took the cup, it is said, and merely asked, 'if his colleague was safe, and if the knights had escaped.' Being told that 'they were safe,' 'It is well,' he said, and drank the poison without faltering, and shortly after breathed his last.

90. Eumenes, who was a man of a kind heart and not without a sense of humour, was accosted one day by a person wearing a cloak, with long hair and a beard reaching down to his waist, who asked for a trifle wherewith to buy bread. Eumenes asked him who and what he was. To which the fellow with an offended air and in a tone of reproof replied, that he was a philosopher: 'and I am surprised,' he added, ' how you came to ask what you can see for yourself.' 'I see,' said Eumenes, 'a beard and a cloak, but I have not seen the philosopher yet. But excuse me, sir, would you be kind enough to tell me, what are the signs by which you think we ought to have known that you were a philosopher?' Thereupon one of the gentlemen present proceeded to tell Eumenes that the man was a worthless good-for-nothing vagabond, a haunter of low pothouses, who was accustomed to assail people with scurrilous abuse if he did not get what he asked for.

But Eumenes simply said, 'Let us give him a few pence, whatever he is, for the sake of humanity, not for the sake of the man,' and forthwith gave him enough to purchase bread for a month.

91. The barbarians received Hannibal's army at the boundary of their country with branches and garlands, furnished cattle for slaughter, guides and hostages; and the Carthaginians marched through their territory as through a friendly land.   When, however, the troops had reached the very foot of the Alps, at the point where the path leaves the Isere, and winds by a narrow and difficult defile along the brook Reclus up to the summit of the St. Bernard, all at once the militia of the Gauls appeared partly in the rear of the army, partly on the crests of the rocks enclosing the pass on the right and left, in the hope of cutting off the train and baggage.   But Hannibal, whose unerring tact had seen in all the courtesies of the barbarians nothing but a scheme to secure at once immunity for their territory and a rich spoil, had, in expectation of such an attack, sent forward the baggage and cavalry and covered the march with all his infantry.

Livy, xxi. 32–37.

92. By this means he frustrated the design of the enemy, although he could not prevent them from moving along the overhanging mountain-slopes, parallel to the march of the infantry, and inflicting very considerable loss by hurling or rolling down stones upon it.   At the 'White Stone,' a high isolated chalk cliff, standing at the foot of the St. Bernard, and commanding the ascent to it, Hannibal encamped with his infantry, to cover the march of the horses and sumpter-animals, laboriously climbing upward throughout the whole night; and amidst continual and very bloody conflicts, he at length on the following day reached the summit of the pass. There on the sheltered plain which spreads to the extent of two-and-a-half miles round a little lake, the source of the Doria, he allowed the army to rest.

Livy, xxi. 32-37.

93. Despondency had begun to seize the minds of the soldiers. The paths that were becoming ever more difficult, the provisions failing, the marching through defiles exposed to the constant attacks of foes whom they could not reach, the sadly thinned ranks, the hopeless situation of the stragglers and the wounded, the object which appeared chimerical to all save the enthusiastic leader and his immediate suite,—all these things began to tell even on the African and Spanish veterans. But the confidence of the general remained ever the same; numerous stragglers rejoined the ranks; the friendly Gauls were near; the watershed was reached, and the view of the descending path, so gladdening to the mountain pilgrim, opened up; after a brief repose they prepared with renewed courage for the last and most difficult undertaking, the downward march. In it the army was not materially annoyed by the enemy; but the advanced season—it was already the beginning of September—occasioned troubles in the descent, equal to those which had been occasioned in the ascent by the attacks of the barbarians.

Livy, xxi. 32-37.

E 2

94. On the steep and slippery mountain slope along the Doria, where the recently fallen snow had concealed and obliterated the paths, men and animals went astray and slipped and were precipitated into the chasms. In fact, towards the end of the first day's march, they reached a portion of the road about two hundred paces in length, on which avalanches are constantly descending from the precipices of the Cramont that overhang it, and where in cold summers snow lies throughout the whole year. The infantry crossed; but the horses and elephants were unable to pass over the smooth masses of ice, on which there lay but a thin covering of freshly fallen snow; and the general encamped above the difficult spot, with the baggage, the cavalry, and the elephants. On the following day the horsemen, by zealous exertion in intrenching, prepared a path for horses and beasts of burden; but it was not until after a further labour of three days with constant reliefs, that the half famished elephants could at length be conducted over.

Livy, xxi. 32–37.

95. When he was now advanced in years, although not afflicted with any disease, he lost the sight of his eyes. This calamity he bore with such patience, that no one ever heard him complain, nor did he attend less on that account to private and public business. He used to come into the amphitheatre when an assembly of the people was being held there, riding in a carriage drawn by a pair of mules, and would say what he had to say from the carriage; and no one considered this as a piece of pride on his part. For nothing insolent or boastful ever fell from his lips. Nay, when he heard his own praises sung as the saviour of his country, he only said, he thanked God who, when wishing to restore Sicily, had chosen him to be the instrument of His work. For he thought that nothing in human affairs was carried on without the will of God.

96. The Roman world was deeply interested in the education of its master. A regular course of study and exercise was judiciously instituted : of the military exercises of riding and shooting with the bow ; of the liberal studies of grammar, rhetoric, and philosophy ; the most skilful masters of the East ambitiously solicited the attention of their royal pupil, and several noble youths were introduced into the palace to animate his diligence by the emulation of friendship. Pulcheria alone discharged the important task of instructing her brother in the arts of government, but her precepts may countenance some suspicion of the extent of her capacity or of the purity of her intentions.

97. Pulcheria taught him to maintain a grave and majestic deportment : to walk, to hold his robes, to seat himself on his throne, in a manner worthy of a great prince ; to abstain from laughter ; to listen with condescension ; to return suitable answers ; to assume by turns a serious or a placid countenance ; in a word to represent with grace and dignity the external figure of a Roman Emperor. But Theodosius was never excited to support the weight and glory of an illustrious name ; and instead of aspiring to imitate his ancestors, he degenerated (if we may presume to measure the degrees of incapacity) below the weakness of his father and his uncle.

98. Those verses you know from the Georgics of Virgil are generally read thus :—

> At sapor indicium faciet manifestns, et ora
> Tristia tentantum sensu torquebit amaro.

But Hyginus (a grammarian of no mean repute, I assure you), in his own commentary on Virgil, stoutly maintains that this is not what Virgil left us, but the true reading is one which he found in a book that had once belonged to Virgil's own family, viz.—

> et ora.
> Tristia tentantum sensu torquebit amaror.

And not only Hyginus but other learned men also agree in this opinion ; for it seems absurd to say 'the taste by the bitter sensation will cause them to make wry faces,' for, say they, the taste is the sensation, and it would be the same as if one said, 'the sensation by the bitter sensation will cause' etc. However, when I read Hyginus's note to my tutor, he was mightily offended at the ugliness and awkwardness of the word amaror. ' By the teeth of Peter,' said he (this is his most solemn form of adjuration), 'I am ready to swear that Virgil never wrote that.' But I, for my part, think that Hyginus is right.

99. It was midday when the deputies arrived at Diego's quarters. The first thing they did was to ask the general to order them something to drink. Wine was brought, which they drank, and then asked for more, to the great amusement of the stately Spanish officers, who witnessed with a smile the absence of etiquette of these simple diplomatists. Then the oldest spoke. 'Our people have sent us to ask what makes you so bold as to invade our country?' Diego replied, 'that he relied on his excellent troops, and that if they liked to see his forces, so that they might take back a trustworthy report to their countrymen, he would give them an opportunity.' He then gave orders that all the regiments should form and march past. The spectacle had its effect. The envoys on their return dissuaded their countrymen from making common cause with the besieged; and the people in the town, after repeated fires, the signal agreed upon, had been lighted on the towers in vain, finding themselves disappointed of their only hope of assistance, surrendered to Diego at discretion.

100. Epaminondas never married. When Pelopidas, who had a good-for-nothing son himself, found fault with him for this, and said that therein he was not doing his duty to his country, Epaminondas replied : ' Take care lest you are doing worse still! for your country, who are going to leave behind you such a son as yours. My family cannot die out. My deeds are my children. I leave behind me the memory of the battle of Leuctra, which will not only survive me, but live for ever.' At the time when the exiles under Pelopidas took Thebes, and drove out the Lacedaemonian garrison, Epaminondas kept himself indoors as long as the massacre of citizens was going on, being unwilling to stain his hands with the blood of his countrymen. For he considered every victory in civil war a curse and a calamity.

101. But a report soon circulated through the camp, at first in secret whispers, and at length in loud clamours, of the emperor's death, and of the presumption of his ambitious minister, who still exercised the sovereign

power in the name of a prince who was no more. The
impatience of the soldiers could not long support a state
of suspense. With rude curiosity they broke into the
imperial tent and discovered only the corpse of Nu-
merian. The gradual decline of his health might have
induced them to believe that his death was natural; but
the concealment was interpreted as an evidence of guilt;
and the measures which Aper had taken to secure his
election became the immediate occasion of his ruin.

Livy, ii. 58; xxviii. 24.

102. Yet even in the transport of their rage and grief,
the troops observed a regular proceeding, which proves
how firmly discipline had been re-established by the
martial successors of Gallienus. A general assembly of
the army was appointed to be held at Chalcedon, whither
Aper was transported in chains as a prisoner and a
criminal. A vacant tribunal was erected in the midst of
the camp, and the generals and tribunes formed a great
military council. They soon announced to the multitude,
that their choice had fallen on Diocletian, commander of
the domestics or body-guards, as the person most capable
of revenging and succeeding their beloved emperor.

Livy, ii. 58. Tacitus, Hist. i. 36; iv. 55.

103. The evening was already far advanced, and the
two armies prepared themselves for the approaching combat at the dawn of day. While the trumpets sounded
to arms, the undaunted courage of the Goths was confirmed by the mutual obligation of a solemn oath, and as
they advanced to meet the enemy, the rude songs which
celebrated the glory of their forefathers were mingled
with their fierce and dissonant outcries, and opposed to

the artificial harmony of the Roman shouts. Some
military skill was displayed by Fritigern to gain the
advantage of a commanding eminence, but the bloody
conflict, which began and ended with the light, was maintained on either side by the personal and obstinate
efforts of strength, valour, and agility.

Livy, ix. 40; xxiii. 24.

104. The legions of Armenia supported their fame in
arms; but they were oppressed by the irresistible weight
of the hostile multitude. The left wing of the Romans
was thrown into disorder, and the field was strewed with
their mangled carcasses. This partial defeat was balanced,
however, by partial success: and when the two armies
at a late hour of the evening retreated to their respective
camps, neither of them could claim the honours or the
effects of a decisive victory. The real loss was more
severely felt by the Romans, in proportion to the smallness of their numbers. But the Goths were so deeply
confounded and dismayed by this vigorous and perhaps
unexpected resistance that they remained seven days
within the circle of their fortifications.

Livy, v. 37. Caesar, *Bell. Gall.* i. 24. 50.

105. At night Ben Estepar withdrew his forces to
an eminence, on the summit of which lay a level plain.
There was a river in the rear; on the other three sides
the plateau terminated in a steep descent. Beneath this
bank, on a lower level, was another plain, which bordered
on a similar ridge, equally hard to climb. To this lower
plain the Moorish captain, when the troops of the Spaniards were drawn up in front of their camp, despatched
some light cavalry and skirmishers. In the meantime

Aguilar rode along the Spanish lines in front of the colours, and pointed out to the men, 'that the enemy having abandoned beforehand all hope of resistance on level ground had taken to the hills, where they stood in view, relying on the strength of their position and not on the prowess of their arms. But the walls of Granada, which Spanish soldiers had scaled, were still higher. Yet neither hills nor citadel, nor the sea itself had formed a barrier to their arms.'

106. Before an assembly thus modelled and prepared, Augustus pronounced a studied oration, which displayed his patriotism, and disguised his ambition. ' He lamented, yet excused, his past conduct. Filial piety had required at his hands the revenge of his father's murder ; the humanity of his own nature had sometimes given way to the stern laws of necessity, and to a forced connexion with two unworthy colleagues : as long as Antony lived, the Republic forbad him to abandon her to a degenerate Roman and a barbarian queen. He was now at liberty to satisfy his duty and his inclination. He solemnly restored the Senate and people to all their ancient rights; and wished only to mingle with the crowd of his fellow-citizens, and to share the blessings which he had obtained for his country !'

Livy, iii. 21 ; xxi. 12.

107. It would require the pen of Tacitus (if Tacitus had assisted at this assembly) to describe the various emotions of the Senate ; those that were suppressed and those that were affected. It was dangerous to trust the sincerity of Augustus ; to seem to distrust it was still more dangerous. The respective advantages of monarchy and a republic have often divided speculative enquirers; the present greatness of the Roman state, the corruption of manners, and the licence of the soldiers, supplied new arguments to the advocates of monarchy; and these general views of government were again warped by the hopes and fears of each individual.

108. Amidst this confusion of sentiments, the answer of the Senate was unanimous and decisive. They refused to accept the resignation of Augustus; they conjured him not to desert the Republic which he had saved. After a decent resistance the crafty tyrant submitted to the orders of the Senate, and consented to receive the government of the provinces, and the general command of the Roman armies, under the well-known names of Pro-consul and Imperator. But he would receive them only for ten years. Even before the expiration of that period, he hoped that the wounds of civil discord would be completely healed, and that the Republic, restored to its pristine health and vigour, would no longer require the dangerous interposition of so extraordinary a magistrate.

109. The devout and fearless curiosity of Julian tempted the philosophers with the hopes of an easy conquest; which, from the situation of their young proselyte, might be productive of the most important consequences. Julian imbibed the first rudiments of the Platonic doctrines from the mouth of Ædesius, who had fixed at Pergamus his wandering and persecuted school. But as the declining strength of that venerable sage was unequal to the ardour, the diligence, the rapid conception of his pupil, two of his most learned disciples, Chrysanthes and Eusebius, supplied, at his own desire, the place of their aged master. These philosophers seem to have prepared and distributed their respective parts ; and they artfully contrived, by dark hints, and affected disputes, to excite the impatient hopes of the *aspirant*, till they delivered him into the hands of their associate, Maximus, the boldest and most skilful master of the Theurgic science.

110. By his hands, Julian was secretly initiated at Ephesus, in the twentieth year of his age.. His residence at Athens confirmed this unnatural alliance of philosophy and superstition. He obtained the privilege of a solemn initiation into the mysteries of Eleusis, which, amidst the general decay of the Grecian worship, still retained some vestiges of their primeval sanctity ; and such was the zeal of Julian, that he afterwards invited the Eleusinian pontiff to the court of Gaul, for the sole purpose of con-summating, by mystic rites and sacrifices, the great work of his sanctification. As these ceremonies were performed in the depth of caverns, and in the silence of night ; and as the inviolable secret of the mysteries was preserved by the discretion of the initiated, I shall not presume to describe the horrid sounds and fiery apparitions which were presented to the senses, or the imagination of the aspirant, till the visions of comfort and knowledge broke upon him in a blaze of celestial light.

111. Protagoras was originally a porter. One day he was carrying a bundle of logs, fastened round with a cord, from the country into Abdera, of which town he was a native. It happened that Democritus, a citizen of the same place, a man highly respected for his worth and his

reputation as a philosopher, was walking out into the country, when he met Protagoras stepping along lightly and easily in spite of the clumsy and unwieldy character of the load he was carrying. Democritus went up to him, and examined with curiosity the packing, and greatly admired the skill with which the logs had been arranged; and asked him to halt for a little while. Protagoras did as he was asked; and Democritus on closer inspection found that the bundle of logs so neatly rounded and compactly tied together by a short cord, was balanced and kept in its place on strictly mathematical principles.

112. Democritus enquired who had packed the wood in that way. He said he had done it himself. Whereupon Democritus asked him to untie it, and put it together again in the same way. When he had done so, Democritus, admiring the skill and cleverness of the man, who was evidently uneducated, exclaimed, ' My young friend, with such natural abilities as yours, I think I can find you something higher and better to do.' So he took him home, and kept him, and paid his expenses, and taught him philosophy; and made him the great man he afterwards became.

113. There is nothing in history which is so improving to the reader as those accounts which we meet with of the deaths of eminent persons, and of their behaviour in that dreadful season. I may also add that there are no parts in history which affect and please the reader in so sensible a manner. The reason I take to be this, there is no other single circumstance in the story of any person which can possibly be the case of every one who reads it. A battle or a triumph are conjunctures in which not one man in a million is likely to be engaged; but when we see a person at the point of death, we cannot forbear being attentive to everything he says or does, because we are sure that some time or other we shall ourselves be in the same melancholy circumstances. The general, the statesman, or the philosopher, are perhaps characters which we may never act in, but the dying man is one whom, sooner or later, we shall certainly resemble.

114. An infant comes into the world in a helpless state, and incapable of the exercise of reason. He gradually improves; his reasoning powers expand as his body grows. His first step is to the vivacity of childhood; his second, to the ardour of youth; his third, to the wisdom of manhood. Here he remains stationary for a time, in the full and vigorous exercise of his rational powers. He then begins to feel himself infirm and in-active; diseases impair his frame, the eye waxes dim, the ear becomes deaf. The enjoyments of life, society, books, all now lose their relish; he bends towards the ground, whence he was taken; his feet can no longer sustain their tottering load; he sinks upon his couch, and dies. He is buried, and the body is gradually resolved into its original dust.—And shall this body live again? Nature answers, No. But in the Gospel an animating voice exclaims: I am the resurrection and the life: he that believeth in Me, though he were dead, yet shall he live!

Cicero, *de Senectute*, § 25.

115. We pass the first years of this life in the shades of ignorance, the succeeding ones in pain and labour, the latter part in grief and remorse, and the whole in error ; nor do we suffer ourselves to possess one bright day without a cloud. Let us examine this matter with sincerity, and we shall agree that our distresses chiefly arise from ourselves. It is virtue alone which can render us superior to fortune ; we quit her standard, and the combat is no longer equal. Fortune mocks us ; she turns us on her wheel ; she raises and abases us at her pleasure ; but her power is founded on our weakness. This is an old-rooted evil, but it is not incurable ; there is nothing a firm and elevated mind cannot accomplish. The discourse of the wise and the study of good books are the best remedies I know of ; but to these we must join the consent of the soul, without which the best advice will be useless.

116. What gratitude do we not owe to those great men who, though dead ages before us, live with us by their works, discourse with us, are our masters and guides, and serve us as pilots in the navigation of life, where our vessel is agitated without ceasing by the storms of our passions ! It is here that true philosophy brings us to a safe port, by a sure and easy passage. Dear friend, I do not attempt to exhort you to the study I judge so important. Nature has given you a taste for all knowledge, but fortune has denied you the leisure to acquire it ; yet whenever you could steal a moment from public affairs, you sought the conversation of wise men ; and I have remarked that your memory often served you instead of books.

117. The prospect of a future state is the secret comfort and refreshment of my soul ; it is that which makes

nature look gay about me ; it doubles all my pleasures,
and supports me under all my afflictions. I can look
at disappointments and misfortunes, pain and sickness,
death itself, and what is worse than death, the loss of
those who are dearest to me, with indifference, so long
as I keep in view the pleasures of eternity and the state
of being in which there will be no fears nor apprehen-
sions, pains nor sorrows, sickness nor separation. Why
will any man be so impertinently officious as to tell me
all this is only fancy and delusion ? Is there any merit
in being the messenger of ill news? If it is a dream,
let me enjoy it, since it makes me both the happier and
better man.

Cicero, Tusc. Quest. i. 40.

118. Friends and fellow-soldiers, the seasonable period
of my departure is now arrived, and I discharge, with the
cheerfulness of a ready debtor, the demands of nature.
I have learned from philosophy how much the soul is
more excellent than the body; and that the separation of
the nobler substance should be the subject of joy, rather
than of affliction.   I have learned from religion, that an
early death has often been the reward of piety ; and I
accept, as a favour of the gods, the mortal stroke that
secures me from the danger of disgracing a character,
which has hitherto been supported by virtue and fortitude.
I die without remorse, as I have lived without guilt.   I
am pleased to reflect on the innocence of my private
life ; and I can affirm with confidence, that the supreme
authority, that emanation of the Divine Power, has been
preserved in my hands pure and immaculate.

Cicero, Tusc. Quest. i. 41 ; de Senectute, § 22.

119. The wisest and best of men, in all ages of the world, have been those who lived up to the religion of their country, when they saw nothing in it opposed to morality, and to the best lights they had of the divine nature. Pythagoras's first rule directs us to worship the gods, 'as it is ordained by law,' for that is the most natural interpretation of the precept. Socrates, who was the most renowned among the heathens, both for wisdom and virtue, in his last moments desires his friends to offer a cock to Æsculapius ; doubtless out of a submissive deference to the established worship of his country. Xenophon tells us, that his prince, whom he sets forth as a pattern of perfection, when he found his death approaching, offered sacrifice on the mountains to the Persian Jupiter, and the Sun, 'according to the custom of the Persians.'

Cicero, *Tusc. Quæst.* i. 42.

120. From such a survey of the miseries that haunt man's progress from the cradle to the grave, we may fairly say that the Thracians were in the right, who, if we believe Herodotus, used to lament when children were born, and to rejoice when they died. They welcomed the termination of life as an end of wretchedness, and a haven of rest ; whilst they regarded its beginning with sorrow, as the entrance into a world of woe and pain. If birth then is a calamity, and death a blessing, who would wish to come into this world to be the victim of lifelong misery ? Who would not rather die, so to gain an immortality of happiness ? And if we would choose this for ourselves as the best of blessings ; why should we pray for anything different for our children and relations ?

F

Can we wish to be better off than those we love so
dearly, or could we desire happiness for ourselves, and
misery for them? No, surely not.

121. Thales being asked how a man might bear ill-
fortune with most ease, answered, ' By seeing his enemies
in a worse condition.' An answer truly barbarous and
unworthy of human nature. Solon lamenting the death
of a son, one told him, 'You lament in vain.' 'Therefore,' said he, ' I lament because it is in. vain.' This was
a plain confession, how imperfect all his philosophy was,
and that something was still wanting. Plato himself
placed happiness in wisdom, health, good fortune, honour
and riches, and held that they who enjoyed all these
were perfectly happy; which opinion was indeed unworthy its owner, leaving the wise and good. man wholly
at the mercy of uncertain chance, and to be miserable
without resource.

Cicero, Tusc. Quæst. i. 10, 43.

122. There is scarcely among the evils of human life
any so generally dreaded as poverty.

Against other evils the heart is often hardened by true
or by false notions of dignity and reputation : thus we
see dangers of every kind faced with willingness, because
bravery, in a good or bad cause, 'is never without its
encomiasts and admirers. But in the prospect of poverty,
there is nothing but gloom and melancholy; the mind
and body suffer together; its miseries bring no allevia-
tions; it is a state in which every virtue is obscured, and
in which no conduct can avoid reproach : a state in
which cheerfulness is insensibility, and dejection sullen-

ness, of which the hardships are without honour, and the labours without reward.

Of these calamities there seems not to be wanting a general conviction; we hear on every side the noise of trade, and see the streets thronged with numberless multitudes, whose faces are clouded with anxiety, and whose steps are hurried by precipitation, from no other motive than the hope of gain.

123. Discretion points out the noblest ends to us, and pursues the most proper and laudable methods of attaining them. Cunning has only private selfish aims, and sticks at nothing which may make them succeed. Discretion has large and extended views, and like a well-formed eye, commands a whole horizon. Cunning is a kind of short-sightedness, that discovers the minutest objects which are near at hand, but is not able to discern things at a distance. Discretion, the more it is discovered, gives a greater authority to the person who possesses it. Cunning, when it is once detected, loses its force, and makes a man incapable of bringing about even those events which he might have done had he passed only for a plain man. Discretion is the perfection of reason, and a guide to us in all the duties of life : cunning is a kind of instinct that only looks out after our immediate interests and welfare.

Cicero, *de Officiis*, iii. 25 ; i. 43.

124. To the solemn question, as to which religion was the true one, the High Priest thus replied : 'No one has applied to the worship of the Gods with greater zeal and fidelity than myself, but I do not see that I am the

better for it ; I am not more prosperous, nor do I enjoy
a greater share of the royal favour.   I am ready to give
up those ungrateful Gods : let us try whether these new
ones will reward us better.'   But there were others of
more reflective minds.   A thane came forward and said,
'To what, O King, shall I liken the life of man ?   When
you are feasting with your thanes in the depth of winter
and the hall is warm with the blazing fire, and all around
the wind is raging, and the snow falling, a little bird
flies through the hall, enters at one door and escapes at
another.   For a moment, while within, it is visible to
the eyes, but it came out of the darkness of the storm,
and glides again into the same darkness.   So is human
life ; we behold it for an instant, but of what has gone
before, or what is to follow after, we are utterly ignorant.
If the new religion can teach this wonderful secret, let
us give it our serious attention.'

125. I shall here relate a Jewish tradition concerning
Moses, which seems to be a kind of parable, illustrating
what I have last mentioned.   That great prophet, it is
said, was called up by a voice from heaven to the top of
a mountain ; where, in a conference with the Supreme
Being, he was admitted to propose to him some questions
concerning his administration of the universe.   In the
midst of this divine colloquy he was commanded to look
down on the plain below.   At the foot of the mountain
there issued out a clear spring of water, at which a
soldier alighted from his horse to drink.   He was no
sooner gone than a little boy came to the same place,
and finding a purse of gold which the soldier had
dropped, took it up and went away with it.

126. Immediately after this came an infirm old man, weary with age and travelling, and having quenched his thirst, sat down to rest himself by the side of the spring. The soldier missing his purse, returns to search for it, and demands it of the old man, who affirms he had not seen it, and appeals to heaven in witness of his innocence. The soldier, not believing his protestations, kills him. Moses fell on his face with horror and amazement, when the Divine voice thus prevented his expostulation : ' Be not surprised, Moses, nor ask why the Judge of the whole earth has suffered this thing to come to pass. The child is the occasion that the blood of the old man is spilt ; but know that the old man whom thou sawest was the murderer of that child's father.'

127. Menippus, the philosopher, was a second time taken up into heaven by Jupiter, when, for his entertainment, he lifted up a trap-door that was placed by his footstool. At its rising there issued through it such a din of cries as astonished the philosopher. Upon his asking what they meant, Jupiter told him they were the prayers that were sent up to him from the earth. Menippus, amidst the confusion of voices, which was so great that nothing less than the ear of Jove could distinguish them, heard the words ' riches, honour,' and ' long life,' repeated in several different tones and languages. When the first hubbub of sounds was over, the trap-door being left open, the voices came up more separate and distinct. The first prayer was a very odd one ; it came from Athens, and desired Jupiter to increase the wisdom and the beard of his humble sup-

pliant. Menippus knew it, by the voice, to be the prayer
of his friend Lycander, the philosopher.

128. The philosopher seeing a great cloud mounting
upwards and making its way directly to the trap-door,
inquired of Jupiter what it meant. ' This,' says Jupiter,
' is the smoke of a whole hecatomb that is offered me
by the general of an army, who is very importunate with
me to let him cut off a hundred thousand men that are
drawn up in array against him. What does the impudent wretch think I see in him, to believe that I will
make a sacrifice of so many mortals as good as himself,
and all this to his glory forsooth? But hark !' says
Jupiter, ' there is a voice I never heard but in time of
danger : 'tis a rogue that is shipwrecked in the Ionian
sea. I have saved him on a plank but three days ago,
upon his promise to mend his manners : the scoundrel
is not worth a groat, and yet has the impudence to offer
me a temple if I will keep him from sinking.'

129. The king had been for some time in a declining
state of health : this had encouraged a saucy astrologer
to foretell his death, and that it should happen before
the year expired. The wise king had more mind to
expose than punish him. So he sent for the man and
talked friendly with him, seeming not to know anything of his insolent prophecy. The king gravely
asked him, ' Whether any future events could be fore-
told by the stars ?' 'Yes, Sir (says the man), without
all doubt.' ' Well ! have you any skill in the art of
foretelling ?' The man affirmed that he had very good
skill. ' Come then,' says the king, ' tell me where you

are to be in the Christmas holidays that are now coming?'
The man faltered at first, and then plainly confessed he
could not tell where. 'Oh!' says the king, 'I am a
better astrologer than you. I can tell where you will
be—in the Tower of London,' and accordingly commanded him to be committed a prisoner thither; and
when he had lain there, till his spirit of divination was
a little cooled, the king ordered him to be dismissed for
a silly fellow.

Cicero, *de Divinat.* ii. c. 23, § 50 sqq.

130. The generality of mankind live in the world
without receiving any kind of delight from the various
scenes of beauty which its order displays. The rising
and setting of the sun, the varying aspect of the moon,
the vicissitude of seasons, the revolution of the planets,
and all the stupendous scenery that they produce, are to
them only common occurrences, like the ordinary events
of every day. They have been so long familiar that they
cease to strike them with any appearance either of magnificence or beauty, and are regarded by them with no
other sentiments than as being useful for the purposes
of human life. We may all remember a period in our
lives when this was the state of our own minds; and it is
probable most men will recollect that the time when
nature began to appear to them in another view, was
when, as boys at school, they were engaged in the study
of classical literature.

Cicero, *Tusc. Quæst.* i. 28.

131. Epictetus makes use of an allusion, which is very
beautiful, and wonderfully proper to incline us to be

satisfied with the post in which Providence has placed
us.   'We are here,' says he, 'as in a theatre, where every
one has a part allotted to him.   The great duty which
lies upon a man is to act his part in perfection.   We
may indeed say that our part does not suit us, and that
we could act another better.   But this,' says the philosopher, 'is not our business.   All that we are concerned
in is to excel in the part which is given us.   If it be
an improper one the fault is not in us, but in Him who
has cast our several parts, and is the great disposer of
the drama.'   The part that was acted by this philosopher
himself was but a very indifferent one, for he lived and
died a slave.

Cicero, de Senectute, § 70.

132. A dervise, travelling through Tartary, having
arrived at the chief city of that province, went into the
king's palace by mistake, thinking it to be a public inn.
Having looked about him for some time, he entered into
a long gallery, where he laid down his wallet, and spread
his carpet, in order to repose upon it after the manner
of the eastern nations.   Before he had lain there long,
some of the guards discovered him, and asked what he
was doing in that place.   To whom when the dervise
had replied that he intended to pass the night in that inn,
the guards angrily told him that the house he was in was
not an inn, but the king's palace.

133. During this debate the king himself by chance
passed through the gallery, and, smiling at the mistake
of the dervise, asked him how he could be so dull as not

to distinguish a palace from an inn. 'O king,' said the dervise, 'give me leave to ask you a few questions. Who lodged in this house when it was first built?' The king replied, 'his ancestors.' 'And who,' said the dervise, 'lodged here last?' The king replied, 'his father.' 'And who now lodges here?' The king told him, 'that he himself did.' 'But who,' rejoined the other, 'will be here after you?' To this last question when the king had answered, 'the young prince his son,' the dervise said, 'therefore, O king, a house that changes its inhabitants so often, and receives such a perpetual succession of guests, you will rightly call not a palace but an inn.'

134. While at a distance from the enemies' frontier, they disperse through the woods, and support themselves with the game which they kill, or the fish which they catch. As they approach nearer to the territories of the nation which they intend to attack, they collect their troops, and advance with greater caution. Even then they proceed wholly by stratagem and ambuscade. They place not their glory in attacking their enemies with open force. To surprise and destroy is the greatest merit of a commander, and the highest pride of his followers. War and hunting are their only occupations, and they conduct both with the same spirit and the same arts. They follow the track of their enemies through the forest. They endeavour to discover their haunts, they lurk in some thicket near to these, and with the patience of a sportsman lying in wait for game, will continue in their station day after day, until they can

rush upon their prey when most secure, and least able to resist them.

135. While engaged in hunting they shake off the indolence peculiar to their nature, and become active, persevering, and indefatigable. Their sagacity in finding their prey, and their address in killing it, are equal. They discern the footsteps of a wild beast, which escape every other eye, and can follow them with certainty through the pathless forest. If they attack their game openly, their arrow seldom errs from the mark ; if they endeavour to circumvent it by art, it is almost impossible to avoid their toils. Their ingenuity, sharpened by emulation, as well as by necessity, has struck out many inventions which greatly facilitate success in the chase. The most singular of these is the discovery of a poison in which they dip the arrows employed in hunting. The slightest wound with those envenomed shafts is mortal. If they only pierce the skin, the blood fixes and congeals in a moment, and the strongest animal falls motionless to the ground.

136. At length Aristodemus himself was dismayed by many visible signs of impending ruin. His daughter too appeared to him as he slept clad in black, and, shewing her wounds, took away his arms and adorned him as for his obsequies with a golden crown and a white robe. Thus certain of his own fate, and of that which he could no longer avert from his country, he slew himself at his daughter's tomb. After his death the hopes of the citizens sank, but not their courage. They chose a new commander, and when they were hard pressed by famine, they made a sally from the walls against the besiegers. But the fates were adverse ; for their bravest leaders fell, and in the twentieth year of the war they fled from the mountains on which they had so long dwelt, leaving their rich fields in the possession of their conquerors. Such was the end of the first Messenian war.

Cicero, de Divinat. i. 46; i. 24; i. 47.

137. The most affecting incident was afforded by the multitude of Christian captives, who were rescued from the Moorish dungeons. They were brought before the sovereigns, with their limbs heavily manacled, their beards descending to their · waists, and their sallow visages emaciated by captivity and famine. Every eye was suffused with tears at the spectacle. Many recognized their ancient friends, of whose fate they had long been ignorant. Some had lingered in captivity ten or fifteen years; and among them were several belonging to the best families in Spain. On entering the presence, they would have testified their gratitude by throwing themselves at the feet of the sovereigns; but the latter, raising them up and mingling their tears with those of the liberated captives, caused their fetters to be removed, and after administering to their necessities dismissed them with liberal presents.

Livy, vii. 28.

138. This proclamation caused great joy : so great in fact that they could not realize it at once.

The multitude refused to credit their own senses, and stood gazing at each other in amazement, wondering whether it was all the delusion of a dream. Such news was indeed too good to be true. Therefore they recalled the messenger and made him repeat the announcement, each one eager to see as well as hear the herald of their freedom. This confirmation of the glad tidings was followed by such a succession of hearty cheers and acclamations, as left no doubt that of all blessings none is more dear to men than liberty. Nor was this a mere transient ebullition of joy. For days it formed the subject of their thoughts and the chief topic of their conversation, and men reflected with gratitude 'That there was one nation in the world, which was ready to sacrifice money, labour, and life for the cause of liberty: and that, not to confer the boon only on contiguous states, or neighbouring populations; but they even cross the sea to put down oppression everywhere, and assert the sovereignty of law, order, and justice.'

139. The water washed some of the crew overboard, and, entering the chinks, drowned others. When the boat had been launched, the young prince was received into it, and might certainly have been saved by reaching the shore, had not his sister, now struggling with death on the larger vessel, implored her brother's assistance, shrieking out that he should not abandon her so barbarously. Touched with pity, he ordered the boat to return to the ship, that he might rescue his sister; and thus the unhappy youth met his death through excess of affection; for the skiff, overcharged by the multitudes who leaped into her, sank, and buried all indiscriminately in the deep. One rustic alone escaped, who, floating all night upon the mast, related in the morning the dismal catastrophe of this tragedy.

140. A few days before his death he seemed to be aware that he would not be long with us, but not so much from any decay or weakness of body, as from an instinctive impression that he was about to depart to his appointed rest. I well remember his giving me warning of this presentiment. It was on a glorious summer evening, and we were taking our usual walk, just as the sun was setting with unusual but mild brilliancy, he stood for a time and watched it in silence and then, ' I shall soon,' he said, ' follow ; may I too set in light and not in clouds and darkness.' His mind remained as fresh as ever even to the last. The very day before he died, he arranged his worldly affairs, and named several to whom he wished memorials to be given : no one was forgotten.

141. But the events of the last year of this struggle plainly showed what Rome would have to fear from a coalition of all the twelve cities. Two of the Roman generals were defeated : one was killed in the battle, and the panic spread to the lines before Veii, and even to Rome itself, where the rumour prevailed that the whole force of Etruria was on its march, that the camp before Veii was actually assailed by the enemy, and that the victorious bands might be expected at any moment to advance on Rome. So great was the alarm that the matrons crowded to the temple to avert by prayers and sacrifices their country's peril, and the Senate resolved to appoint a Dictator.

142. Meanwhile Charles, satisfied with the easy and almost bloodless victory which he had gained, and advancing slowly, with the precaution necessary in an enemy's country, did not yet know the whole extent of his own

good fortune. But at last, a messenger despatched by
the slaves acquainted him with the success of their noble
effort for the recovery of their liberty; and at the same
time deputies arrived from the town in order to present
him the keys of their gates, and to implore his protection
from military violence. While he was deliberating concerning the proper measures for this purpose, the soldiers,
fearing lest they should be deprived of the booty which
they had expected, rushed suddenly and without orders
into the town, and began to kill and plunder without
distinction. It was then too late to restrain their cruelty,
their avarice, or their licentiousness. Above thirty thousand of the innocent inhabitants perished on that unhappy day, and ten thousand were carried away as slaves.

143. Gulliver thus relates how he dragged the ships of
the Blefuscudians into the harbour of Lilliput : 'the emperor and his whole court stood on the shore expecting the
issue of this great adventure. They saw the ships move
forward in a large half moon, but could not discern me,
who was up to my breast in water. When I advanced to
the middle of the channel, they were yet more in pain
because I was under water to my neck. The emperor
concluded me to be drowned, and that the enemy's fleet
was approaching in a hostile manner; but he was soon
eased of his fears, for the channel growing shallower every
step I made, I came in a short time within hearing, and
holding up the end of the cable by which the fleet was
fastened, I cried in a loud voice, Long live the most
puissant emperor of Lilliput !'

144. We had one dangerous place to pass, as to which
our guide told us, if there were any more wolves in the

country we should find them there; and this was in a
small plain surrounded with woods on every side, and a
long narrow defile, or lane, which we were to pass to get
through the wood, and then we should come to the
village where we were to lodge. It was within half an
hour of sunset when we entered the first wood, and
a little after sunset when we came into the plain. We
met with nothing in the first wood, except that in a little
plain within the wood, which was not above two furlongs
over, we saw five great wolves cross the road, full speed
one after another, as if they had been in chase of some
prey, and had it in view; they took no notice of us, and
were gone and out of our sight in a few moments. Upon
this our guide, who by the way was a wretched faint-
hearted fellow, bid us keep in a ready position, for he
believed there were more wolves a-coming. We kept our
arms ready, and our eyes about us, but we saw no more
wolves till we came through that wood, which was near
half-a-league, and entered the plain. As soon as we
came into the plain, we had occasion enough to look
about us. The first object that we met with was a dead
horse ; that is to say, a poor horse which the wolves had
killed, and at least a dozen of them at work.

145. The consul Flaminius now at last broke up from
his position and followed the enemy. Hannibal laid
waste the country on every side with fire and sword, to
provoke the Romans to a hasty battle ; and leaving Cor-
tona on his left untouched on its mountain seat, he approached the lake of Thrasymenus, and followed the road
along its north eastern shore, till it ascended the hills
which divide the lake from the basin of the Tiber.

Flaminius was fully convinced that Hannibal's object was not to fight a battle, but to lay waste the richest part of Italy: had he wished to engage, why had he not attacked him when he lay at Arretum, and while his colleague was far away at Ariminum? With this impression he pressed on his rear closely, never dreaming that the lion would turn from the pursuit of his defenceless prey, to spring on the shepherds who were dogging his steps behind.

146. The consul had encamped in the evening on the side of the lake, just within the present Roman frontier, and on the Tuscan side of Passignano; he had made a forced march, and had arrived at his position so late that he could not examine the ground before him. Early the next morning he set forward again; the morning mist hung thickly over the lake and the low grounds, leaving the heights, as is often the case, quite clear. Flaminius, anxious to overtake his enemy, rejoiced in the friendly veil which thus concealed his advance, and hoped to fall upon Hannibal's army while it was still in marching order, and its columns encumbered with the plunder of the valley of the Arno. He passed through the defile of Passignano, and found no enemy: this confirmed him in the belief that Hannibal did not mean to fight. Already the Numidian cavalry were on the edge of the basin of the Tiber: unless he could overtake them speedily, they would have reached the plain; and Africans, Spaniards, and Gauls, would be rioting in the devastation of the garden of Italy.

Livy, xxii. 3 sqq.

147. We have it on the authority of a learned doctor that a number of men were sent down by the king into an old mine, long ago deserted, to explore it, and ascertain its productiveness, and find out whether the greed of the ancients had left aught for those who came after. He says they went down well supplied with lights, and remained below several days. They traversed passage after passage until they were tired. At last they reached an enormous cavern and beheld, not without a shudder, a vast expanse of sluggish water, as large as the lakes of the upper earth ; the roof above lost in height and darkness. I was glad to find that avarice is not a vice peculiar to our day : that the vaunted contentment and simplicity of the early world did not prevent our ancestors from ransacking the bowels of the earth, and groping for gold in the mysterious darkness of the central deeps.

148. As they left their homes, they smote their breasts and wrung their hands, and raised their weeping eyes to heaven in anguish ; and this is recorded as their plaint : 'Oh, Malaga ! city renowned and beautiful ! where now is the strength of thy castles? where the grandeur of thy towers? of what avail have been thy mighty walls for the protection of thy children ? Behold them driven from thy pleasant abodes, doomed to drag out a life of bondage in a foreign land, and to die far from the home of their infancy ! What will become of thy old men and matrons, when their grey hairs shall be no longer reverenced ! what will become of thy maidens, so delicately reared, and tenderly cherished, when reduced.to hard and menial servitude ! Sons are separated from their fathers, husbands

G

from their wives, and tender children from their mothers. They will bewail each other in foreign lands; but their lamentations will be the scoff of the stranger.   Oh, Malaga! city of our birth! who can behold thy desolation, and not shed tears of bitterness?'

149. But the good knight looking over the river perceived about two hundred Spanish horse making straight for the bridge, which they would have gained with little resistance; and that would have been the total destruction of the French army.   He desired his companion to go and collect some men as quickly as possible to defend the bridge, or they would all be lost, and promised to do his best to keep the enemy in play till his return.   He then went lance in hand to the bridge, on the other side of which were the Spaniards already prepared to pass: but he, levelling his lance, charged those who were already on the bridge, so that three or four of them were overthrown and fell into the water.   This done, he was so fiercely assailed that had he not been an excellent knight he could not have checked them.   But, backing his horse against the barrier of the bridge, that they might not get in his rear, he defended himself so well with his sword that the Spaniards thought he was more than man.   And he maintained his post till Le Basco, his companion, arrived with about a hundred men-at-arms, who made the Spaniards abandon the bridge.

Livy, ii. 10.

150. But the ingenuity of Columbus suggested a happy artifice, that not only restored, but augmented the high opinion which the Indians had originally entertained of

the new-comers. By his skill in astronomy he knew that
there was shortly to be a total eclipse of the moon. He
assembled all the principal persons of the district around
him on the day before it happened, and after reproaching
them for their fickleness in withdrawing their affection
and assistance from men whom they had lately revered,
he told them that the Spaniards were servants of the
Great Spirit who dwells in heaven, who made and
governs the world; that he, offended at their refusing to
support men who were the objects of his peculiar favour,
was preparing to punish this crime with exemplary
severity, and that very night the moon should withhold
her light, and appear of a bloody hue, as a sign of the
divine wrath, and an emblem of the vengeance ready to
fall upon them.

> Tacitus, *Annals*, i. 28.
> Livy, xliv. 37.

151. Many of the Indians were alarmed at the pre-
diction, others treated it with derision—all, however,
waited to see what would happen when night arrived.
When they beheld a dark shadow stealing over the moon,
they began to tremble; as the moon was covered more
and more their fears increased, and when they saw a
mysterious darkness over the whole face of nature, there
were no bounds to their terror. Seizing upon whatever
provisions were at hand, they hurried to the ships, threw
themselves at the feet of Columbus, and implored him to
intercede with his God to withhold the threatened calamities, assuring him they would thenceforth bring him whatever he required. Columbus shut himself up in his cabin,
as if to commune with the Deity, and remained there

during the increase of the eclipse, the forests and shores all the while resounding with the howlings and supplications of the savages. When the time was come for the light to reappear, he came forth and informed the natives that his God had deigned to pardon them; in sign of which he would withdraw the darkness from the moon.

Tacitus, *Annals*, i. 28.
Livy, xliv. 37.

152. Animals in their generation are wiser than the sons of men: but their wisdom is confined to a few particulars, and lies in a very narrow compass. To use an instance that comes often under observation: with what caution does the hen provide herself a nest in places unfrequented, and free from noise and disturbance! When she has laid her eggs, what care does she take in turning them frequently, that all parts may partake of the vital warmth! When she leaves them to provide for her necessary sustenance, how punctually does she return before they have time to cool, and become uncapable of producing an animal! When the birth approaches, with how much nicety and attention does she help the chick to break its prison, not to mention her covering it from the injuries of the weather, providing it proper nourishment, and teaching it to help itself; nor to mention her forsaking the nest, if after the usual time of reckoning the young one does not make its appearance! A chymical operation could not be followed with greater art or diligence than is seen in the hatching of a chick; though there are many other birds that shew infinitely greater sagacity in all the forementioned particulars.

Cicero, *de Naturâ Deorum*, ii. 52.

153. But at the same time the hen, that has all this seeming ingenuity (which is indeed absolutely necessary for the propagation of the species), considered in other respects is without the least glimmerings of thought or common sense. She mistakes a piece of chalk for an egg, and sits upon it in the same manner: she is insensible of any increase or diminution in the number of those she lays; she does not distinguish between her own and those of another species, and when the birth appears of never so different a bird, will cherish it for her own. In all these circumstances, which do not carry an immediate regard to the subsistence of herself or her species, she is a very idiot.

There is not in my opinion anything more mysterious in nature than this instinct in animals, which thus rises above reason and falls infinitely short of it.

Cicero, de Naturâ Deorum, ii. 47 sqq.

154. There is a river called Astræus flowing midway between Beræa and Thessalonica, in which are produced certain spotted fish—the Macedonians must give you their name—whose food consists of insects which fly about the river. These insects are dissimilar to all other kinds found elsewhere; they are unlike wasps, nor would one naturally compare them with the flies called ephemera, nor do they resemble bees; but they possess characters common to all these creatures; for they are as impudent as flies, as large as the anthedon, of the same colour as wasps, and they buzz like bees. The natives call this insect the hippurus. As these flies float on the top of the water in pursuit of their food, they attract the notice of the fish which swim therein. When a fish spies one of these insects on the top of the water, it swims quietly underneath it, taking care not to agitate the surface, lest it should scare away the prey.

155. So approaching it, as it were, under its shadow, the fish opens its mouth and gulps it down, just as a wolf seizes a lamb from the flock, or an eagle a goose from the yard; and having done this it swims away beneath the ripple. The fishermen are aware of all this, but do not use these flies for bait, because handling would destroy their natural colour, injure the wings, and spoil them as lures. On this account the insect is in ill repute with the fishermen, who cannot make use of it. They manage to circumvent the fish however by the following clever piscatorial device. They cover a hook with purple wool, and upon this they fasten two feathers of a waxy colour, which grow underneath a cock's wattles. They have a reed six feet long and a fishing-line of about the same length. They drop this bait upon the water, and the fish being attracted by the colour becomes extremely excited, and proceeds to meet it, anticipating from its beautiful appearance a most delicious repast. But as, with extended mouth, it seizes the prey, it is held by the hook, and being captured meets with a very sorry entertainment.

Cicero, de Naturâ Deorum, ii. 49.

156. The satrap sent him a message pretending that he had himself fallen under the displeasure of Cambyses, and saw no hopes of safety but in the protection of Polycrates : ' Save me,' he said, ' and share my treasures; with them you may be master of Greece; if you doubt their amount send a trusty servant, and satisfy yourself by his report.' Polycrates caught at the bait : his messenger went, and came back from Sardis with a description of the satrap's treasury, which so inflamed his master's cupidity that, in spite of all the warnings of his friends and the entreaties of his daughter, he resolved to make a journey to Sardis himself. He set out with a numerous train, but when he arrived at Magnesia on the Mæander, he was arrested by order of Orœtes, and hung upon a cross.

157. The Grecian fleet, as we have seen, had staid among the Cyclades, to punish the islanders who had aided the barbarians. Themistocles seized the opportunity of enriching himself at their expense. He first demanded a contribution from Andros : and when the Andrians refused it, he told them that the Athenians had brought two powerful gods to second their demand, Persuasion and Force. The Andrians replied that they also had a pair of ill-conditioned gods, who would not leave their island, nor let them comply with the will of the Athenians, Poverty and Inability. The Greeks laid siege to Andros ; but it made so vigorous a defence, that they were at length compelled to abandon the attempt, and returned to Salamis.

Cornelius Nepos, *Themistocles.*

158. The Spaniards, while thus employed, were surrounded by many of the natives, who gazed in silent admiration upon actions which they could not comprehend, and of which they did not foresee the consequences. The dress of the Spaniards, the whiteness of

their skins, their beards, their arms, appeared strange
and surprising. The vast machines in which they had
traversed the ocean, that seemed to move upon the
waters with wings, and uttered a dreadful sound resembling thunder, accompanied with lightning and smoke,
struck them with such terror, that they began to respect
their new guests as a superior order of beings, and concluded that they were the children of the Sun, who had
descended to visit the earth.

Cæsar, *de Bello Gallico*, iv. 23.

159. When with infinite toil they had climbed up the
greater part of that steep ascent, Balboa commanded his
men to halt, and advanced alone to the summit, that he
might be the first who should enjoy a spectacle which
he had so long desired. As soon as he beheld the
South Sea stretching in endless prospect below him, he
fell on his knees, and lifting up his hands to Heaven,
returned thanks to God, who had conducted him to a
discovery so beneficial to his country and so honourable
to himself. His followers observing his transports of
joy, rushed forward to join in his wonder, exultation,
and gratitude. They held on their course to the shore
with great alacrity, when Balboa advancing up to the
middle in the waves with his buckler and sword, took
possession of that ocean in the name of the king his
master, and vowed to defend it with these arms against
all his enemies.

Cæsar, *de Bello Gallico*, iv. 25.

160. The houses of Sardis were chiefly of wicker-work,
and those which were built of bricks, were thatched with
reeds. A soldier during the pillage set fire to a house :

the flames soon spread through the town. The inhabitants, driven out of their houses, rushed in a body to the market-place on the Pactolus, their last retreat, and with the courage of despair defended themselves against the enemy. The Athenians and their allies, kept at bay in the midst of a burning city, began to think their own situation dangerous. They therefore resolved to make a timely retreat, and hastily retraced their march over the ridge of Tmolus, and down the vale of the Cayster. They had not long left Sardis before the whole force of the province, which had been promptly levied on the news of the invasion, came up to protect the capital. It overtook them in the Ephesian territory, where a battle took place in which they were defeated ; the Ionian troops dispersed among their cities ; and their allies sailed home to Athens.

Livy, xxvi. 27.

161. Holguin seeing four canoes, crowded with people, rowing hastily across the lake, gave chase, and soon overtook them. He was preparing to attack the largest of them, when, all at once, the rowers dropped their oars, and those on board, throwing down their arms, conjured him with tears to forbear, as the emperor was there. Holguin eagerly seized his prize, and the emperor, with a dignified composure, gave himself up into his hands, requesting only that no insult might be offered to the empress or his children. When brought before Cortes, he appeared neither with the sullen fierceness of a barbarian, nor with the dejection of a suppliant. ' I have done,' said he, ' what became a monarch. I have defended my people to the last extremity. Nothing

now remains but to die.   Take this dagger,' laying his
hand on one which Cortes wore, 'plant it in my breast,
and put an end to a life which can no longer be of use.'

Cæsar, *de Bello Gallico*, vii. 50.

162. Others collected their subjects in order to oppose
his progress, and he quickly perceived what an arduous
undertaking it was to conduct such a body of men
through hostile nations, across swamps and rivers and
woods which had never been passed. but by straggling
Indians.   But by sharing in every hardship with the
meanest soldier, by appearing the foremost to meet
every danger, by promising confidently to his troops
the enjoyment of honour and riches superior to the
most successful of their countrymen, he inspired them
with such enthusiastic resolution that they followed him
without murmuring.   When they had penetrated a good
way into the mountains, a powerful chief appeared in
a narrow pass with a numerous body of his subjects to
obstruct their progress.   But men who had surmounted
so many obstacles despised the opposition of such feeble
enemies.   They attacked them with impetuosity, and
having dispersed them with much ease and great slaughter, continued their march.

Cæsar, *de Bello Gallico*, iv. 30.

163. His attendants advised him to wait until he had
made preparations of men and money ; to which he only
returned, 'They that love me will follow me.'   He entered the ship in a violent storm : which the mariners
beholding with astonishment at length in great humility
gave him warning of the danger ; but the King com-

manded them instantly to put off, and not be afraid, for he had never in his life heard of any king that was drowned. In a few days he drove the enemy from before the city, and took the count himself prisoner ; who, raging at his defeat and calamity, exclaimed, 'That this blow was from fortune ; but valour could make reprisals, as he should shew if he ever regained his liberty.'

Cæsar, *de Bello Gallico*, iv. 23.

164. It was the last that was ever seen of them upon earth. They all went down together, in the midst of the fight, and were never heard of more. The battle terminated, as usual in those conflicts of mutual hatred, in horrible butchery, hardly any of the patriot army being left to tell the tale of their disaster. At least four thousand were killed, including those who were slain on the field, those who were suffocated in the marshes or the river, and those who were burned in the farm-houses where they had taken refuge. It was uncertain which of these various modes of death had been the lot of Count Louis, his brother, and his friend. The mystery was never solved. They had probably all died on the field ; but stripped of their clothing, with their faces trampled upon by the hoofs of horses, it was not possible to distinguish them from the less illustrious dead. It was the opinion of many that they had been drowned in the river ; of others that they had been burned.

Livy, i. 16.

165. In the meanwhile Eteonicus received intelligence of the event of the battle by means of a boat which had

been kept in readiness for the purpose. To deceive
Conon, he directed the men who brought the news to sail
out again in the most private manner, and presently to
return to the camp with garlands on their heads, and
shouts of joy, announcing that Callicratidas had conquered,
and that the whole Athenian armament was destroyed.
When the boat came back, he himself made a public
sacrifice of thanksgiving for the victory: but he gave
orders to the captains of the fleet to sail away as soon as
possible to Chios, and advised the merchants who had
been attracted to his camp to embark their property as
secretly and speedily as they could, and accompany the
retreating squadron. The wind favoured their flight. He
himself, after setting fire to his camp, led the land force
across the island to Methymna.

166. Questioned as to the relations subsisting between
themselves and the natives of Britain, the Belgæ asserted
that many of their own race had emigrated from Gaul
during the preceding century and established themselves
beyond the white cliffs just visible on the horizon. They
spoke of a population believed by them to be aboriginal,
upon whom they had intruded themselves, and in whose
seats they had gradually fixed their abodes. This primi-
tive people they described as peculiarly rude and barbarous in their social habits. They were almost destitute
of clothing, and took a grotesque pleasure in tattooing
their bodies with blue woad. They lived almost entirely
on milk and flesh, the toil or skill required even for fishing
was distasteful to them; and dwelling apart or congre-
gating in a few hovels, with a wooden stockade round
them, and screened by forests, mountains, or morasses,

they possessed nothing which could deserve the name
of a city.

Cæsar, *de Bello Gallico*, v. 12 sqq.

167. There was at this time in the neighbourhood of
Mount Olympus, a boar of enormous size, that used to
sally forth from his lair in the mountain and work great
damage among the farms of the Mysians. Oftentimes the
Mysians had gone out to attack him; but so far from
hurting the monster they only suffered great loss themselves. At last they sent messengers to King Crœsus,
and thus they prayed : ' Sire, a monstrous boar hath appeared in our country, and worketh us great mischief, and
do what we will we cannot slay him. Now therefore we
entreat thee, let thy son, and a chosen band of young
men, and hounds go with us, that so we may drive him
out of the country.' Such was the request they made.
But Crœsus remembering the words of his dream, answered them thus.

168. ' Say not a word more about my son, for I will
not let him go with you. He is lately married, and that
gives him enough to think about now. Yet I will send
a picked band of young men, and a full pack of hounds :
and I will command those who go to do their best in
helping you to drive the creature out of your land.' So
spake the king; and the Mysians were satisfied with his
promise. But just at this juncture the young prince came
in, having heard the request of the Mysians. When
therefore Crœsus refused to let his son go with them,
the young man addressed him thus, ' Father,' he said,
' it has always heretofore been our glory and delight to

go forth and earn honour in battle and the chase, but now thou hast debarred me from both of these, and that, not because thou hast observed anything craven or cowardly in me.

169. 'But now, how shall I dare to look people in the face when I walk in the streets? What will the citizens think of me? What will my young bride think of me? To what kind of a husband will she think she is mated? Do let me go then to the hunt, or any how show me good reason why it is better for me not to go.' To this Crœsus made answer, 'My boy, it is not that I have seen any sign of cowardice or faintheartedness in thee, that I do this: but a vision appeared to me in my sleep, and said that thy life would be short, for that thou shouldest be killed by an iron spear point. Looking therefore to this dream, I hastened thy marriage, and will not let thee go on this quest, but keep watch over thee, if by any means I may keep thee alive during my lifetime. For thou art my only son, since I look upon my other son as lost to me because he is deaf and dumb.'

170. Then the young man replied, 'Father, thou mayest be pardoned after seeing such a vision for keeping watch over me, yet thou dost not read the dream aright, and its meaning hath escaped thee. I will explain it. Thou sayest the vision said I should be slain by an iron spear point. What hands then hath a boar, or where is the spear point thou fearest? If it had said I should die by tooth or tusk or ought of that kind, then wouldst thou have had good cause to do as thou dost. But now it said by a spear. Since then we are not going to fight with

men, let me go.' And Crœsus answered, ' My son, thou
hast conquered. Thine is the right interpretation of the
dream. Thou hast convinced me, I retract my word, and
give thee leave to go to this hunt.'

171. These several reports reached the senators who
were assembled in the Temple of Faith. P. Cornelius
Scipio Nasica, a man of the highest nobility, of great
landed property, and of a stern and determined temper,
called upon P. Mucius, the consul, to take instant and
vigorous measures for the destruction of the tyrant. To
this Mucius answered, that he would not set the example
of shedding blood, nor destroy any citizen without trial ;
but if the people were seduced or terrified by Gracchus
into any illegal resolutions, he should consider such resolutions to be of no authority. Nasica then exclaimed,
' The consul deserts the republic ; let those who wish
to preserve it follow me.' At once the senators arose,
wrapped their gowns around their left arms as a shield,
and proceeded in a body towards the capitol.

172. Siccius Dentatus was known as the bravest man in
the army that had been sent against the Sabines. He had
taken an active part in the civil contests, and was now
suspected, by the Decemvirs in command of the army,
of plotting against them. Accordingly they determined
to get rid of him, and for this end they sent him out
as if to reconnoitre, with a party of soldiers, who were
secretly instructed to murder him. Having discovered
their design, he resolved to defend himself to the last.
More than one of his assailants fell, and the rest stood
round him, not daring to come near him, when one

wretch climbed up the rock behind him, and crushed
the brave old man with a massive stone. But the army
learned the circumstances of his death, and the generals
only prevented a sedition by honouring him with a magnificent funeral.

Livy, iii. 43.

173. The Pompeians were too much dispirited to make
any resistance. Shivered once more at the first onset,
they poured in broken masses over hill and plain. But
Cæsar was not yet satisfied. Allowing a part of his
troops only to return to the camp, he led four legions
in hot pursuit by a shorter or better road, and drew them
up at the distance of six miles from the field of battle.
The fugitives finding their retreat intercepted, halted on
an eminence overhanging a stream. Cæsar set his men
immediately to throw up intrenchments, and cut off their
approach to the water. This last labour was accomplished before nightfall ; and when the Pompeians perceived that their means of watering were intercepted, they
listened to the summons of the heralds who required
their surrender.

Cæsar, de Bello Civili, iii. 97.

174. In the meantime the enemy had gone into winter-
quarters. When Laurentius learnt this, he determined
to take measures for surprising them, as he felt he was
no match for their forces, if notice should reach them
beforehand of his approach. There were two routes
from Teheran, where he was quartered, by which the
encampment of his adversaries could be reached. The
shorter of the two lay across the desert, which was un-
inhabited from lack of water : this was a ten days' march.

The ordinary route made a bend, and was as long again, but afforded means of subsistence in plenty. If he took the latter, however, he felt sure that the enemy would get news of his approach, before he had accomplished a third part of the journey: while by forced marches through the desert, he hoped to be able to fall upon the foe unawares. .

He resolved on the latter course, and made his preparations accordingly. He ordered a great number of water bottles and sacks to be collected; next a sufficient quantity of fodder; and lastly rations for ten days, ready cooked, so as to avoid the necessity of having fires in the camp. He did not tell a soul the secret of his destination.

175. After the prisoner had made this statement he was asked by the king whether the information he gave was from hearsay, or from his own knowledge, and his answer was, that he had been a shepherd, and had himself traversed every one of the paths he told them of; that he had been twice taken prisoner, once in Lycia, by the Persians, and now again by his interrogator. At this, there flashed across the king's mind the recollection of a prophecy, which had been made to him once, when consulting the oracle at Delphi: 'that a Lycian should be his guide on the way to Persia.' Therefore, having promised the man a rich reward, he bids him array himself in the Macedonian uniform, and with God's blessing shew the way. 'However steep and difficult it might be, he himself and a few more would make the journey, unless, forsooth, he fancied that where he had gone for the sake of his flock, Alexander would shrink from going for the sake of glory.' The captive continued to insist on

H

the difficulty of the route, especially for men in full armour. But the king replied, 'Take my word for it, that not one of those who undertake this enterprise will refuse to go where you lead.'

176. On receiving this news, Alexander halted, and gave his men repose for four days, so that they should go into action fresh and vigorous. He also fortified his camp, and deposited in it all his military stores, and all his sick and disabled soldiers; intending to advance upon the enemy with the serviceable part of his army perfectly unencumbered. After this halt, he moved forward, while it was yet dark, with the intention of reaching the enemy, and attacking them at break of day. About half-way between the camps there were some undulations of the ground, which concealed the two armies from each other's view. But, on Alexander's arriving at their summit, he saw by the early light the Persian host arrayed before him. Some of the officers were for attacking instantly at all hazards, but the more prudent opinion of Parmenio prevailed, and it was determined not to advance farther till the battle-ground had been carefully surveyed.

177. It appears that destiny is not so much a thing that gives no warning as a thing that cannot be avoided; for they say that wondrous signs and appearances presented themselves before the death of Cæsar. Many men, all of fire, were seen contending against one another in the sky; a certain slave emitted a flame from his hand, and appeared to the spectators to be burning, but when the flame went out the man had sustained no harm: and while Cæsar himself was sacrificing, the heart of the victim could not be found. The following stories also are told by many: that a certain seer warned him to be on his guard against great danger on that day of the month of March which the Romans call the Ides : and when the day had arrived Cæsar on his way to the Senate house saluted the seer and jeered him, saying, 'Well, the Ides of March are come :' but the seer mildly replied, ' Yes, they are come, but they are not yet over.'

> Cicero, *de Naturâ Deorum,* ii. 3. § 7.
> „ *de Divinatione,* i. 46. § 104.
> Suetonius, *Jul. Cæs.* 81.

178. When Cæsar entered, the Senate rose to do him honour, and some of the party of Brutus stood around his chair at the back, and others presented themselves before him, as if their purpose was to support the prayers of Tillius Cimber on behalf of his exiled brother : and they all joined in entreaty, following Cæsar as far as his seat. When he had taken his seat, and was rejecting their entreaties, and as they urged them still more strongly, began to shew displeasure towards them individually, Tillius taking hold of his toga with both hands pulled it downwards from the neck, which was the signal for the attack. Casca was the first to strike him on the neck with his sword, a blow neither mortal nor severe, for, as was natural at the beginning of so bold a deed, he was confused, and Cæsar turning round seized the blade and held it fast.

> Suetonius, *Jul. Cæs.* 81.

179. And it happened that at the same moment he who was struck cried out in the Roman language, ' You villain Casca, what are you doing ?' and he who had

given the blow cried out to his brother in Greek,
' Brother, help !' Such being the beginning, those who
were not privy to the conspiracy were prevented by
consternation and horror at what was going on either
from flying or going to aid, and they did not even ven-
ture to utter a word. And now each of the conspirators
bared his sword, and Cæsar being hemmed in all round,
in whatsoever direction he turned meeting blows and
swords aimed against his eyes and face, driven about
like a wild beast, was caught in the hands of his enemies;
for it was arranged that all of them should take a part in
and taste of the deed of blood.

Suetonius, Jul. Cæs. 81.

180. Accordingly Brutus also gave him one blow in the
groin. It is said by some authorities, that he defended
himself against the rest, moving about his body hither
and thither, and calling out, till he saw that Brutus had
drawn his sword, when he pulled his toga over his face
and offered no further resistance, having been driven
either by chance or by the conspirators to the base on
which the statue of Pompey stood. And the base was
drenched with blood, as if Pompey was directing the
vengeance upon his enemy who was stretched beneath
his feet and writhing under many wounds ; for he is
said to have received three and twenty wounds. Many
of the conspirators were wounded by one another, while
they were aiming so many blows against one body.

Suetonius, Jul. Cæs. 81.

181. After the Governor's order was executed, two old
men appeared before him, one of them with a large cane

in his hand, which he used as a staff. 'My lord,' said
the other, who had none, 'some time ago I lent this man
ten gold crowns to do him a kindness, which money he
was to repay me on demand. I did not ask him for
it again for a good while, lest it should prove a greater
inconvenience to him to repay me than he laboured
under when he borrowed it. However, perceiving that
he took no care to pay me, I have asked him for my
due; nay, I have been forced to dun him hard for it.
But still he did not only refuse to pay me again, but
denied he owed me anything, and said, "that if I lent
him so much money he certainly returned it."'

Cicero, de Officiis, iii. 14.

182. 'Now, because I have no witnesses of the loan,
nor he of the pretended payment, I beseech your lord-
ship to put him to his oath, and if he will swear he has
paid me, I will freely forgive him before God and the
world.' 'What say you to this, old gentleman with the
staff?' asked Sancho. 'Sir,' answered the old man, 'I
own he lent me the gold; and since he requires my
oath, I beg you will be pleased to hold down your rod
of justice, that I may swear upon it how I have honestly
and truly returned him his money.' Thereupon the
Governor held down his rod, and in the meantime the
defendant gave his cane to the plaintiff to hold, as if
it hindered him, while he was to make a cross and
swear over the judge's rod: this done, he declared
that it was true the other had lent him ten crowns, but
that he had really returned the same sum into his own
hands; and that, because he supposed the plaintiff had
forgotten it, he was continually asking him for it.

183. The great Governor, hearing this, asked the creditor what he had to reply? He made answer, that since his adversary had sworn it he was satisfied; for he believed him to be a better Christian than to offer to forswear himself, and that perhaps he had forgotten he had been repaid. Then the defendant took his cane again, and, having made a low obeisance to the judge, was immediately leaving the court, which when Sancho perceived, reflecting on the passage of the cane, and admiring the creditor's patience, after he had studied awhile with his head leaning over his stomach, and his forefinger on his nose, on a sudden he ordered the old man with the staff to be called back. When he was returned, 'Honest man,' said Sancho, 'let me see that cane a little. I have a use for it.' 'With all my heart,' answered the other; 'Sir, here it is,' and with that he gave it him. Sancho took it, and giving it to the other old man, ''There,' said he, 'go your ways, and Heaven be with you, for now you are paid.'

184. 'How so, my lord?' cried the old man; 'do you judge this cane to be worth ten gold crowns?' 'Certainly,' said the Governor, 'or else I am the greatest dunce in the world. And now you shall see whether I have not a headpiece fit to govern a whole kingdom upon a shift.' This said, he ordered the cane to be broken in open court, which was no sooner done, than out dropped the ten crowns. All the spectators were amazed, and began to look on their Governor as a second Solomon. They asked him how he could conjecture that the ten crowns were in the cane? He told them, that having observed how the defendant gave it to the plaintiff to hold while he took his oath, and then swore that he had truly returned him the money into his own hands, after which he took his cane again from the plaintiff : this considered, it came into his head that the money was lodged within the reed. From whence may be learned, that though sometimes those that govern are destitute of sense, yet it often pleases God to direct them in their judgment.

185. The lad, in answer to their enquiry, recounted the popular legend, that Pontius Pilate, proconsul of Judea, had here found the termination of his impious life ; having, after spending years in the recesses of that mountain, which bears his name, at length in remorse and despair, rather than in penitence, plunged into the dismal lake which occupies the summit. Whether water refused to do the executioner's duty upon such a wretch, or whether, his body being drowned, his vexed spirit continued to haunt the place where he committed suicide, Antonio did not pretend to explain. But a form was often, he said, seen to emerge from the gloomy waters, and go through the action of one washing his hands ; and when he did so, dark clouds of mist gathered first round the bosom of the Infernal Lake, (such it had been styled of old,) and then wrapping the whole upper part of the mountain in darkness, presaged a tempest or hurricane, which was sure to follow in a short space.

186. The Roman army in Sicily was rescued from its perilous position by the self-devotion of Cædicius. He went to the general in command and represented to him that unless the force was immediately extricated, it must be surrounded and cut to pieces by the Carthaginians. 'And this is what I think must be done,' he said, 'if you would save the Roman arms from destruction. You must send five hundred soldiers to that mound you see yonder, rising steep and craggy in the centre of the enemies' position, with orders to capture and hold it. It will follow that all the bravest and most active of the enemy's soldiers will rush to meet and oppose them; and so there will be a desperate struggle about the mound, in which all our five hundred that I spoke of will be cut to pieces. In the meantime, while the foe is entirely occupied with this one affair, and busy with the slaughter, you will have time to get our main army out of the fatal trap. There is no other way of safety than this.'

187. The general replied, 'Your advice sounds honest and prudent; but where shall we find a man to lead your five hundred to that place in the very heart of the enemy?' 'If you cannot find any one else,' says the officer, 'I will lead the forlorn hope. I put my life at the disposal of my country and my general.' The general thanked the officer and paid him a well-deserved compliment. Being put in command of a band of five hundred Cædicius explained to them, whither he was going to take them, and for what purpose. 'We are bound, my men,' he said, 'to get to yonder hill, but we are not bound to get back again! Let us die if so be we must, and by our death deliver the army from its perilous position.' Then, without a hope of escaping, fired by the love of glory and the wish to save their comrades, they all set forth.

188. The enemy at first were astonished to see this

band of heroes coming straight at them, and could not make out what their object was. But when it became apparent that they were marching to occupy the mound, the Carthaginian commander despatched against them the best men of all his army, both horse and foot. The Romans were surrounded, and made a brave resistance. The struggle was long doubtful. At length numbers prevailed. The five hundred fell to a man, pierced with the sword, or overwhelmed by missiles. Meantime their general, while the fight was going on, managed to reach an elevated position where he was quite safe. Providence rewarded the officer according to his bravery. For it so happened that although struck in various places, he did not receive a single wound in a vital part. He was found among the dead covered with gashes, but eventually got well; and many a time afterwards did good service for his country.

189. There was a stream of no great size near the camp of the enemy, from which both the Romans and the Spaniards used to get water ; pickets being stationed on either bank to enable them to do so in safety. All was quiet at the river, when one morning about nine o'clock, a mule escaping from its owners, ran away and made for the other bank. Three soldiers from the Roman side were following through the water, which was about knee deep, when a couple of Basques dashed in and dragged the animal from the mid-channel to their own side. One of the Basques was immediately slain, the mule was recovered, and the soldiers began to return to their own quarters. There was a guard of eight hundred Basques on the other side of the river. A few of them,

at first, indignant at seeing their fellow-countryman cut down before their eyes, crossed the river in pursuit of their slayers. Soon more followed ; at last the whole force joined in, and a general conflict ensued with the Roman outpost on the other bank.

190. In his flight from Mutina, D. Brutus having learnt that the soldiers sent by Antonius to kill him were close at hand, hid himself in a wood, together with a few of his followers, to escape being put to death. However the soldiers discovered their retreat, and here S. Terentius, practising a loyal deception, and aided by the darkness of the place, gave out that he was Brutus, and offered his own throat to the butchers. But being recognised by Furius, who had been commissioned to slay Brutus, he was unable to avert his friend's massacre by his own death ; and so by compulsion of fortune he continued to live. By the nobleness of the intention, and not by the failure of the event ought Terentius' devotion to his friend to be judged. For although it was not granted him to carry out his resolve to die instead of Brutus ; yet, as far as in him lay, he sacrificed himself and saved his friend.

191. Many of the most illustrious men of ancient Rome passed their lives in poverty. It was their pride not only not to covet riches, but to despise them. Attilius Regulus commanding the Roman legions in Africa, had defeated the Carthaginians in several battles, and receiving the intelligence that his command had been prolonged on account of his many brilliant successes, he wrote to the consuls to say that his steward, who had

managed his estate (seven acres was the extent of it) had
died; and that the slave he had hired, finding his opportunity, had run away, and carried off the tools of hus-
bandry; wherefore he besought them that they would
appoint a successor to him in Africa, lest if his land was
left deserted, there would be nothing to support his wife
and children. The consuls laid his request before the
Senate, who ordered that the property which Regulus
had lost should be made good at the public expense, that
the field should be ploughed, and maintenance provided
for his wife and children.

192. The practice of charity should be guided by good
judgment. A wise man will bestow charity on the good,
or at least on those he will be able to make good. He
will choose the most deserving; for inconsiderate muni-
ficence is but a waste of money. They are mistaken who
think that philanthropy is an easy business. It is a very
difficult thing, if you determine to use discretion, instead
of throwing money broadcast. Some I will succour because they do not deserve to feel the pinch of poverty.
To some I will not give, although they are in want; because, however much I give them they will be in want
still. To some I will offer help, on others I will force it.
What matters it whether they are slaves or freemen who
are in want? Wherever a human being is, there is room
for a good act. I will give to a poor man, if he is honest.
I shall not aim to get either gain, or gratification, or glory
for my charity. I will give that I may do my duty
towards my neighbour. Although the recipient of my
bounty has no means of proving his gratitude, yet I shall
have acted up to my principles.

193. Although a man ought to be desirous of possessing all the virtues, yet is there nothing which a generous nature would more desire than to feel and to shew gratitude. This was a characteristic of Augustus that he wished to appear grateful to all who had done him a kindness. One day an old soldier, who was in trouble, having been summoned to defend a lawsuit, made his appearance, and appealed to the emperor to protect him. Augustus immediately selected one of his suite, an advocate, and told him to undertake the case of the litigant. At this the veteran exclaimed in a loud voice, 'Nay, then, your majesty, when your life was in jeopardy at Actium, I did not go and look for a substitute; but I fought for you myself. Look here;' and at the same time he disclosed his scars. Cæsar blushed, and undertook the man's defence in person.

194. Then the child went to Pampeluna to take leave of the king, his uncle. The king made him great cheer, and tarried him there a ten days, and gave to him great gifts, and to his men. Also the last gift that the king gave him proved his death : I shall shew you how.

When this gentleman should depart, the king drew him apart into his chamber, and gave him a little purse full of powder, which powder was such that if any creature living did eat thereof, he should incontinent die without remedy. Then the king said, ' Gaston, fair nephew, ye shall do as I shall shew to you. Ye see how the Count of Foix, your father, wrongfully hath your mother, my sister, in great hate; whereof I am sore displeased, and so ought ye to be: howbeit, to perform all the matter, and that your father should love your mother again, to that intent ye shall take a little of this powder, and put it on some meat that your father may eat it ; but beware that no man see you.'

195. The child who thought that all the king said to him had been true, said, 'Sir, it shall be done as ye have devised.' And so he departed from Pampeluna and returned to Orthez. The count, his father, made him good cheer, and demanded tidings of the King of Navarre, and what gifts he had given him ; and the child shewed him how he had given him divers, and shewed him all except the purse with the powder.

Ofttimes this young Gaston and Juan, his bastard brother, lay together, for they loved each other like brethren, and were like arrayed and apparelled, for they were near of a greatness and of one age. And it happened on a time as their clothes lay together on their bed, Juan saw a purse at Gaston's coat, and said ' What thing is this that ye bear ever about you?' Whereof Gaston had no joy, and said, ' Juan give me my coat, ye have nothing to do therewith.' And all that day after that Gaston was pensive.

196. And it fortuned a three days after, as God would that the count should be saved, Gaston and his brother Juan fell out together, playing at tennis, and Gaston gave him a blow, and the child went into his father's chamber and wept. And the count as then had heard mass, and when the count saw him weep, he said 'Son Juan, what ailest thou ?' ' Sir,' quoth he, ' Gaston hath beaten me, but he were more worthy to be beaten than me.' ' Why so ?' quoth the count, and incontinent suspected nothing. ' By my faith, Sir,' said he, ' since he returned out of Navarre, he beareth privily at his breast a purse full of powder. I wot not what it is, nor what he will do therewith; but he hath said to me once or twice, that my lady, his mother, should shortly be again in your grace, and better beloved than ever she was.' 'Peace,' quoth the count, 'and speak no more, and shew this to no man living.' 'Sir,' said he, 'no more I shall.'

197. The count then entered into imagination, and so came to the hour of his dinner; and he washed and sat down at his table in the hall. Gaston his son was used to set down all his service, and to taste the viands. And when he had set down the first course, the count cast his eyes on him, and saw the strings of the purse hanging at his bosom. Then his blood changed, and he said, 'Gaston, come hither, I would speak with thee in thine ear.' And the child came to him, and the count took him by the bosom, and found out the purse, and with his knife cut it from his bosom. The child was abashed, and stood still, and spake no word, and looked as pale as ashes for fear, and began to tremble. The Count of Foix opened the purse, and took of the powder, and laid it on a trencher of bread, and called to him a dog, and gave it him to eat; and as soon as the dog had eaten the first morsel, he turned his eyes in his head, and died incontinent.

198. And when the count saw that, he was sore displeased, and also he had good cause, and so rose from the table, and took his knife, and would have stricken his son. Then the knights and squires ran between them, and said, 'Sir, for God's sake, have mercy and be not so hasty; be well informed first of the matter, ere you do any evil to your child.' And the first word that the

count said, was, 'Ah, Gaston! traitor! for to increase
thine heritage that should come to thee, I have had war
and hatred of the French King, of the King of England,
of the King of Spain, of the King of Navarre, and of the
King of Arragon, and as yet I have borne all their malice,
and now thou wouldest murder me ; it moveth of an evil
nature ; but first thou shalt die with this stroke.' And so he
stepped forth with his knife, and would have slain him.

199. There is a little bird called the tufted-lark. It
lives among the cornfields, and builds its nest in time
enough for the young ones to be fledged before the
harvest time arrives. Now it happened that one of these
birds had settled in a field where the corn was more
forward than usual. And so, when the grain began to
turn yellow, the young birds had not got their feathers
yet. Thereupon when she was going to get food for her
chickens, she warned them that if anything out of the
common was done or said in her absence they were to
take notice of it and tell her when she returned. After
this comes the owner of the crop and calls his grown up
son, and says, 'Yonder grain is ripe, d'ye see, and wants
cutting. Therefore to-morrow as soon as it is light, go
get our friends to come, and lend a hand to get the crop
in.' This said, he went away.

200. And when the lark came back the little ones all
in a flutter began to chatter around her and beseech their
mother to make haste directly and take them away to
some other place. 'For the master,' said they, 'has sent
to ask his friends to come at daybreak, and begin the
reaping.' The mother bids them be quite at their ease,

'For if the master,' says she, 'has put off the reaping on his friends, the crop will not be gathered to-morrow, nor is there need that I should take you away to-day.' So the next day the mother flies off to get food. The master is there watching for the friends he had applied to. The sun gets hot, and nothing is done, and no friends were forthcoming. Then the farmer turns to his son again, and says, 'Those friends of ours are great dawdlers: let us rather go and beg our kinsmen, and relations, and neighbours to come to-morrow early to begin the reaping.'

201. This too the little ones in a great fright report to their mother. Again their mother bids them to be without fear or anxiety. 'Kinsmen and relations,' she tells them, 'are not generally so complaisant as to hurry up to do work without any delay, on short notice. Only mind and take notice if anything more is said.' Another day came. The bird went out again to get food. The kinsmen and relations put off giving the assistance they were asked for. At last, therefore, the master says to his son, 'Good-bye to friends and relations,' says he, 'bring two sickles to-morrow morning; I will take one, and you shall take the other, and we will reap the corn to-morrow ourselves with our own hands.' When the mother heard from the little ones that the farmer had said this, 'It is time,' she said, 'to get up and be off; what he said will be done to-morrow without doubt. For now the matter rests with the owner, and does not depend on help asked from others.'

And so the lark changed her nest, and the crop was reaped by the master.

202. A great number of people having come one day,

'during the siege of Leyden, to Adrian, exclaiming that he ought either to give them food or deliver the town into the hands of the enemy, 'I have solemnly sworn,' he replied, 'that I will never surrender myself, or my fellow citizens, to the cruel and perfidious Spaniard; and I will sooner die than violate my oath. I have no food, else would I give it you. But, if my death can be of use to you, take, tear me in pieces, and devour me: I shall die with satisfaction, if I know that by my death I shall for one moment relieve you from your direful necessity.' By this extraordinary answer, the people struck with astonishment, were silent, and their fury was for some time appeased.

203. I had it from the mouth of a certain Captain Moreno whom Don Henry had sent out on an expedition to discover the sources of the Nile. He said that he and his company had penetrated a long way into the country, having been helped on their way by the king of Abyssinia, and being supplied with passports to the neighbouring kings. 'At the furthest point we reached,' he said, 'we came upon enormous marshes, which have no outlet that the natives even know of. To cross them indeed is hopeless; the waters are so beset with reeds and matted weeds, that you can neither wade through on foot, nor pierce them in a boat. No craft large enough to hold more than one could float upon that choked and muddy swamp. There we saw an arched canyon, or tunnel, out of which a great volume of water flowed. Whether that is the fountain head of the Nile, or a tributary, whether it takes its rise there, or emerges there after running

I

a long way underground, I cannot help thinking that it
is supplied from some vast subterranean reservoir.'

204. At that time there were two Grecians about
P. Crassus, called Hieronymus and Nicomachus : they
both counselled him to steale away with them, and flie to
Ischenæ, a town not far from thence, which took the
Romans' part.   But Publius answered them, that there
was no death so cruel as could make him forsake those
that died for his sake.   When he had so said, wishing
them to save themselves, he embraced them, and took
his leave of them : and being very sore hurt with an
arrow through one of his hands, commanded his shield-
bearer to thrust him through with a sword, and so turned
his side to him for the purpose.   And most part of the
gentlemen that were of that company, slew themselves
with their own hands.   The rest were slain by the
Parthians, who struck off P. Crassus's head and placed
it on a pike, and returned straight to set upon the elder
Crassus.

205. The boldness of these boatmen in shooting the
rapids is something marvellous.   Two of them will take a
small canoe, and one of them steers while the other bales.
After tossing about for a considerable time among the
mad swirling billows and conflicting currents of the river,
they enter the narrows, and avoiding the rocks that jut out
from the sides, are shot along with the full volume of the
river, guiding their skiff with the paddle as it darts along
the slope.   Presently, to the unspeakable terror of the
lookers on, the head of the boat dips, and down they go.
You give them up for lost, you think they must be over-

whelmed and drowned under the mass of waters, when lo! they are floating several hundred yards below the place where they took the plunge, as if they had been shot out of a cannon. The fall of water instead of causing the boat to sink, drives it on the faster into the smooth reach further down.

206. As we were on our way home from Cyprus, we arrived at Brindisi; where we went ashore, and took a stroll in the town. On the quay we saw a book-stall with a number of old books for sale, and I hastened with great eagerness to inspect them. They proved to be all Greek story books, full of marvels, and romances, and travellers' tales, and incredible histories. Some of them were by authors of repute such as Ctesias, Polystephanus, and Hegesias. The volumes themselves were soiled and shabby from long neglect, by no means an attractive looking set. However, I went in and asked the price, and being taken by the astonishing and unexpected smallness of the price asked, I bought several for an old song, as they say; and spent the next two nights in skimming them all through.

207. In those books I came upon things of this kind, that the remotest of the Tartar tribes who live under the north star, eat human bodies, and thrive on that diet, and are called cannibals. Likewise that there are men in the same part of the world, with only one eye in the middle of the forehead, who are called Arimaspians; and that there are others in those same regions of remarkable velocity, who have their feet turned backwards, instead of forwards like the rest of mankind. It was stated also that there are certain tribes in the interior of Africa, who have the power of bewitching people; for instance, if they chance to praise anything excessively, the beauty of a tree, say, or the abundance of a crop, or if they remark what a sweet child! what a splendid horse! or what fine cattle! all the objects named are sure to die suddenly, without any other apparent reason.

208. His eldest son, the heir of his house and honours, Don Pedro de Cordova, a youth of great promise, fought at his side. He had just received a severe wound on his head from a stone, and a javelin had pierced through his leg. With one knee resting on the ground, however, he still made a brave defence with his sword. The sight was too much for the father, and he implored him to suffer himself to be removed from the field. 'Let not the hopes of our house be crushed at a single blow,' said he, 'go my son, live as becomes a Christian knight—live and cherish your desolate mother.' All his entreaties were fruitless, however; and the gallant boy refused to leave his father's side, till he was forcibly borne away by the attendants, who fortunately succeeded in bringing him in safety to the station occupied by the Count of Urena.

209. Volumnius had been an intimate friend of Lucullus. When he had seen Lucullus put to death, by the order of Antonius, although he might have saved his life by flight, he clung to his dead friend, bursting out into tears and lamentations, and his excessive affection proved the cause of his death. For, impatient of his obstinate lamentation, the guards dragged him off to

Antony's quarters. When Volumnius came into Antonius' presence, he cried out, 'Order me to be taken away directly to the corpse of Lucullus, and there be put to death. He is destroyed and I have no right to survive him, I who advised him to undertake the fatal campaign against thee.' Antonius granted his request without demur. He was led to the spot as he had requested, and there he seized the hand of Lucullus and devoured it with kisses, and passionately embraced the body of his friend. After which, he presented his neck to the sword of the executioner.

210. Eudemus, a Cyprian, when on his way to Macedonia came to Pheræ, a town of Thessaly, at that time under the sway of Alexander, a cruel tyrant. In this town Eudemus fell sick, so that all the doctors despaired of his recovery. While he lay ill, there appeared to him in his sleep a beautiful youth, who told him that he would soon get well again, and that the tyrant Alexander would die in a few days, and Eudemus himself after five years would return home. And sure enough the first two predictions were speedily fulfilled, Eudemus got well, and the tyrant was assassinated by his wife's brothers. But at the end of the fifth year, when he was hoping to return to Cyprus, according to the dream, he fell in battle before the walls of Syracuse. And so the dream was interpreted to mean, that when the soul of Eudemus left his body, he returned home.

211. It was the custom at Rome for the censors to set a mark of disapprobation against the name of any citizen on their list who was guilty of immorality or gross

misconduct.   An instance is related of their somewhat
puritanical strictness.   It was gravely deliberated whether
they should thus stigmatize a man, who, having been
invited by a friend to appear in court as his legal adviser,
while standing before the bench had actually yawned out
loud in his worship's face.   The offender narrowly escaped
punishment, the censor considering it a sign of a wandering, dreamy, inattentive mind, and a flagrant contempt
of court.   However, when the man swore on oath that
he could not help it, do what he would, that he was a
victim to yawning, which almost amounted to a disease
with him, he was released from the threatened stigma.
The following example too is given by Sabinus of their
strictness.   The censors were once going through the
muster roll of the knights, when they spied a lean and
sorry hack, very badly groomed, while the rider looked
as plump and as smart as you please.   'How comes it,
sir,' they demanded, 'that you are so much better cared
for than your horse?'   'Because,' quoth the knight, 'I
take care of myself, but my man takes care of the horse.'

212.   A certain Pythagorean had bought a pair of shoes
from a shoemaker on credit.   A few days afterwards he
came to the shop to pay the money.   But finding it shut
up he began to knock at the door, whereupon a head appeared at a neighbouring window, and the following
words were addressed to him.   'What is the good of
wasting your labour ?   The shoemaker you are looking for
is dead and buried.   This is a bad job for us who think we
shall never see him any more ; but makes no difference to
you who know that he will rise again.'   This was a cut
at the Pythagoreans, who believed in Metempsychosis, or

the transmigration of souls. So our friend the philosopher, not altogether reluctantly, takes back the three
or four shillings, which he had brought with him to pay
for the shoes, jingling the money in his hand as he went
along. Presently he reflected that he was gloating over
his paltry gain, and, his conscience disapproving of the
silent pleasure he derived from not repaying the debt, he
said thus to himself, 'The shoemaker still lives for you.
Pay back what you owe.' So he returned to the shop,
and pushing the coins in through a crack in the door, let
them drop, and so made atonement for his dishonest
thought.

213. A shepherd, in pursuing a goat which had strayed
from his flock, having discovered a secret path by which
it was possible to ascend to the top of the rock, came
with the intelligence to Maurice. A small band of chosen
soldiers, under the command of George of Mecklenburg,
was instantly ordered to follow this guide. They set out
in the evening, and clambering up the rugged track with
infinite fatigue and danger, they reached the summit un-
perceived : and at an hour which had been agreed on,
when Maurice began the assault on the one side of the
castle, they appeared on the other, ready to scale the
walls, which were feeble in that place, because it had
been hitherto deemed inaccessible. The garrison, struck
with terror at the sight of an enemy on a quarter where
they had thought themselves perfectly secure, immediately
threw down their arms.

Livy, ix. 24; xxiv. 46.

214. Sylla after dislodging the garrisons in Euboea

and Bœotia, routed the entire force of the king in two battles, one at Chæronea, and the other at Orchomenus. He then crossed over to Asia Minor and defeated Mithridates himself. And the war might have been ended then, if Sylla had not been more anxious to secure a hasty triumph, than a permanent success. The situation brought about by him in Asia was this. A treaty was made with the people of Pontus. Bithynia was taken from the king and transferred to Nicomedes; and Cappadocia to Ariobarzanes; and thus Asia once more became Roman. Mithridates however was only checked. Their defeat instead of crushing, inflamed the courage of the Pontic people. The king having been in a manner cheated out of his Asiatic dominions, refused to acknowledge the right of another to what had once been his, and endeavoured to recover the lost provinces by force of arms. As a fire imperfectly extinguished will blaze out again with greater violence, so did he set to work to collect a larger army, and at length invaded Asia by land and sea with the whole power of his kingdom.

215. Cyzicus is a famous city on the shores of the Propontis, and, with its citadel, its fortifications, its harbour, and towers built of marble, forms a conspicuous ornament of those parts. Against this city Mithridates had concentrated all his forces, as being no less important than Rome itself. But the inhabitants were encouraged to hold out against him by the report of a messenger, who told them that Lucullus was coming. The messenger, (but the story is a strange one,) had swum through the midst of the enemy's ships, supported by bladders, and steering and propelling himself

with his feet : looking, to those who saw him from afar,
like some monster of the deep. The face of affairs now
changed. The besiegers began to suffer from famine,
and famine was succeeded by pestilence. The king
withdrew, but Lucullus followed, and came up with him,
and inflicted such a blow that the waters of the Granicus
and Æsepus ran red with blood. Knowing the greediness
of the Romans, the king cunningly took advantage of it,
and commanded his men to scatter money and valuables
on the way, in order to delay the pursuit.

216. His flight was no less disastrous by sea, than it
had been on land. The fleet, consisting of more than
a hundred ships, with all his heavy stores and munitions
of war, was overtaken by a storm, which inflicted such
terrible damage, that it crippled him more than a seafight
would have done. It looked as if Lucullus had made
a compact with the winds and waves to fight for him,
and had handed over the king to those elements for destruction. All the resources of a once powerful kingdom
were now exhausted, but his courage rose with misfortune.
Therefore having appealed to the various nations, he
involved nearly the whole of the East and the North in
his own downfall. The Iberians, Caspians, Albanians,
and both the Armenias were stirred up to join him ;
and all these states were taxed by Fortune to contribute
glory, fame, and titles to her favourite Pompey. For
Pompey, seeing all Asia in a ferment, fresh outbreaks
everywhere, and one petty ruler assuming the offensive
after another, determined not to wait until they had
united their forces. He made a bridge of boats, and
crossed the Euphrates, the first who ever did, and

having overtaken the king in Armenia, crushed him in
a single battle.

217. Amidst the darkness of the night an Athenian
messenger on horseback arrived at the camp of the
Lacedæmonians, instructed to ascertain what was passing
there, and to ask Pausanias for the last directions.   For
in spite of the resolution taken after formal debate that
each division of the Grecian army should withdraw simul-
taneously to the island, the Athenian generals still mis-
trusted the Lacedæmonians, and doubted whether after
all they would act as they had promised.   The Athenian
herald found the Lacedæmonians stationary in their position, and the generals in hot dispute with Amompharetus,
who despised the threat of being left alone to make head
against the Persians, and when reminded that the resolution of retiring had been taken by general vote of the
officers, took up with both hands a vast rock fit for the
hands of Ajax or Hector, and cast it at the feet of
Pausanias, saying : ' This is my pebble wherewith I give
my vote not to run away from the strangers.'

218. The people of Tarentum, who had called in the
aid of king Pyrrhus against the Romans, finding, when
too late, that they had got a master instead of an ally,
bewailed their luck with outspoken complaints, especially
when they were warmed up with wine.   Therefore Pyrrhus
sent for a number of them who were charged with having
spoken about him at a banquet in uncomplimentary
terms.   The danger that threatened them was averted by
the frank and ingenious confession of one of the party.
For on the king's asking whether they had really used

the language, which had been reported to him, he said,
'Yes, your Majesty, we said that, and if the wine had not
run short, the language reported to you would have been
a joke to what we were going to say about you.' Thereupon Pyrrhus, preferring to lay the blame on the wine
rather than on the men, laughed, and let them go.

219. When Pyrrhus, on his way back from Sicily, was
sailing past the Locrian coast, he stopped and plundered
the temple of Proserpine, and having placed the treasure
on ship-board, himself continued his journey overland.
Well, what happened? The next day his fleet was shattered
by a terrible storm, and all the ships which carried the
consecrated property were driven back on the shores
of Locri. Taught by this disaster that there is a God
above us, he ordered all the money to be collected and
restored to the treasury of Proserpine's temple. However,
he never prospered again. He was driven out of Italy,
and died an ignoble death. For in a night attack upon
Argos he received a slight wound from the spear of a
young Argive. The lad's mother, a poor old woman,
was on the roof of her house watching the fighting : who,
seeing Pyrrhus charging with all his might the author of
the wound, and fearing for her son's life, seized a tile, and
poising it with both hands, hurled it down upon the head
of the king. Pyrrhus fell wounded from his horse, and
was despatched by one Zopyrus.

220. Alp Arslan defeated and took prisoner Romanus
Diogenes, husband of Eudocia, the empress of Constan-
tinople. He treated his prisoner with extreme kindness,
and is said to have asked him at their first conference,

what he would have done if fortune had reversed their lot. 'I would have given thee many a stripe,' was the unwise and virulent answer. This expression of haughtiness, however, excited no resentment in the brave and generous conqueror. He only smiled and asked Romanus, what he expected would be done to him? 'If thou art cruel,' said the emperor, 'put me to death; if vainglorious, load me with chains and drag me to the capital; if generous, grant me my liberty.' Alp Arslan was neither cruel nor vain-glorious; he released his prisoner.

221. A body of Roman cavalry had been defeated by the Cimbrians at the river Athesis, and were flying panic-stricken towards Rome, having deserted the pro-consul Catulus. The son of Scaurus was one of the runaways. His father therefore sent a messenger to tell him, 'that he would rather have found his dead body on the field of battle, than see him back again under the slur of that disgraceful flight; and therefore, degenerate son that he was, he had better keep out of sight of his incensed father.' The young man, when he heard the message, unable to bear the shame, turned against his own breast the sword which he had failed to use against the foe, and died by his own act.

222. Sobieski gave the word to charge: the Polish cavalry, sword in hand, bore right upon the Vizir, whose station was pointed out by the standard. They dashed in the enemy's foremost ranks, and penetrated to the numerous squadrons which surrounded him. None but the Spahis disputed the victory; the rest, Wallachians, Moldavians, Tartars, even the Janissaries, shewed no good will to the cause, the result of that hatred and contempt of their general which all felt. He would have re-established their confidence by shewing kindness and courage; but it was then too late. He addressed the Pacha of Buda, and other chiefs; they kept silence in despair. 'And you,' he said to the Tartar chief, 'will not you help me?' The Khan replied that he knew the king of Poland, and that there was no safety from him but in flight; of which he immediately set the example.

223. The rebel chieftain, cunning as he was, was taken by a stratagem of Decimus, who promised the king to cut him off, if his majesty would give him permission to effect his purpose in any way he pleased, without fear of punishment, and would give him his hand upon it, as their manner is. Having received this assurance, he collects an army, as if against the king, and gains the friendship of Brutius, without however seeing him; he harries the lands of the king, and takes much spoil, a part of which he gives to his retainers, and part he sends to Brutius. In like manner he delivers over several castles to Brutius. By continuing to act in this way for a long time he persuaded the rebel that he was engaged in serious hostilities against the king. But to prevent Brutius from having any suspicion of a plot, he was careful never to hold conference with him, or even to come into his sight. While keeping at a distance he so managed this friendship, that the two seemed to be bound together, not so much by mutual good offices, as by a common hatred of the king.

224. At length he sends word to Brutius that the time has come for collecting larger forces, and taking the field against the king : and begs him to come to a meeting at any spot he might choose to name. So a time and place of meeting were agreed upon. To this place Decimus repaired with one attendant, in whom he placed great confidence, a few days before the time ; and there buried a number of swords in different spots, marking each spot carefully. On the day appointed they met, unattended, and after some time spent in discussing plans, separated. When Brutius had got a little way off, Decimus, before rejoining his friends, for fear of exciting suspicion, came back to the place, and sat down where one of the swords was hidden, as if he was tired and was resting. Then he called Brutius back, pretending there was something he had forgotten to say. Meanwhile he picked up the sword, unsheathed it, and concealed it under his cloak, and, when Brutius came up, said that as he was going away he had noticed a spot within sight of where they were, suited for pitching a camp. He then pointed to a place, and when the other turned to look at it, stabbed him in the back ; and killed him before any one could come to his rescue. Thus a man who had himself taken many by stratagem, but never a one by perfidy, was himself taken by a pretence of friendship.

225. The envoys, who had not yet been dismissed, on the news of the victory, were summoned before the Senate. There the spokesman is related to have said, ' that they had been sent as ambassadors by their countrymen to make peace between the Romans and Perseus, because the war was both burdensome and oppressive to the whole of Greece, and expensive and ruinous to the Romans themselves. That Fortune had acted kindly, since, by ending the war by other means, it had given them an opportunity of congratulating the Romans on a glorious victory.' So spake the Rhodian envoy. The rejoinder of the Senate was as follows: ' That the Rhodians had not been influenced by the advantage of Greece, nor by anxiety about the expenses of the Roman people, in sending that embassy, but had acted in the interests of Perseus. For if their motive had been what they pretended, they ought to have sent their ambassadors when Perseus, having led an army into Thessaly, was during the space of two years besieging some of the Greek cities, and terrifying others with threats of war. But the Rhodians had not said a word about peace then.'

226. My language, too, is unpolished. I reck little of that. Virtue shines by its own light. It is they, my adversaries, who need the trick of eloquence to hide their vile acts. I never learnt Greek. Why truly I had little inclination to get that kind of learning which had done so little towards making its teachers honest men. But I have learnt other accomplishments far more serviceable to the state : to smite the foemen ; to mount guard ; to dread nothing except dishonour ; to bear heat and cold alike ; to sleep on the bare ground ; and to endure at the same time hunger and fatigue.

227. By conduct like this our forefathers gained immortal honour, both for themselves and their country : while our aristocracy of to-day, proud of their ancestors, though so unlike them in character, despise us who take them for our models, and demand of you all public honours, not on account of personal merit but as theirs by right.   Arrogant men! but widely mistaken!   Their ancestors left them everything in their power to bequeath, their wealth, their titles, their renown.   Their virtue they did not leave them, nor indeed could they, for virtue can neither be given, nor received as a gift.   They hold me to be mean and ill-bred, because I cannot entertain elegantly, cannot prate about 'Art,' and pay no higher wages to my cook than to my steward.   All this I readily own. For I have learnt from my father and other venerable persons that refinement is for women, hard work for men : and that arms are more ornamental than fine furniture.

228. Good agriculture depends upon industry rather than upon expense.   C. Furius Cresinus managed to get larger crops from his very small plot of ground than his neighbours did from their extensive farms, and therefore became an object of great jealousy, because it was thought that he charmed away the produce of other peoples' fields into his own by means of witchcraft.   He was therefore summoned to take his trial on a certain day.   So, fearing that a verdict would be given against him, he brought with him into court all his farm implements.   He also led forward his daughter, a fine strong girl, healthy-looking and neatly clad, and produced his iron tools of good workmanship, his heavy spades, ponderous ploughs, and plump oxen.   'There,' said he, 'gentlemen, those are my charms; but I cannot shew you, nor bring into court my days of toil, and nights of unrest and anxious thought.' He was unanimously acquitted.

229. Laino, whose base is washed by the waters of the Lao, was defended by a strong castle, built on the opposite side of the river, and connected by a bridge with the town. All approach to the place by the high road was commanded by this fortress. Gonsalvo obviated this difficulty, however, by a circuitous route across the mountains. He marched all night, and fording the waters of the Lao about two miles above the town, entered it with his little army before break of day, having previously despatched a small corps to take possession of the bridge. The inhabitants, startled from their slumbers by the unexpected appearance of the enemy in their streets, hastily seized their arms, and made for the castle on the other side of the river. The pass, however, was occupied by the Spaniards; a fierce struggle ensued; many were slain, the rest were taken prisoners; and the Spaniards remained masters of both the castle and the town.

230. For some days he fixed his quarters there, examining the site of the city from every side: and he discovered that it had not been selected without good reason for a royal stronghold. It is situated on a hill sloping towards the south-west. It is surrounded by swamps of impassable depth, both in summer and winter, formed by the overflow of the neighbouring lakes. In that part of the marsh which is nearest the city, there stands, like an island, a fortress built on enormous earthworks, solid enough to support a wall, and secure from the sapping of the neighbouring lagoon. From a distance it looks as if it was joined to the city by the wall. In reality it is separated by a river, which is crossed by a bridge: so that if attacked from without it affords no access in any quarter, nor if the king wishes to keep any one prisoner there, is there any way out except by a bridge easily guarded. The king's treasury was there. But at the time I speak of only three hundred talents were found in it, which had been sent to Ariston, but intercepted on their way.

231. In order to avoid occasion of anger, it is expedient not to see and not to hear everything. Where ignorance is bliss 'tis folly to be wise. You don't wish to have your temper ruffled? Then don't be inquisitive. The man who asks what other people say about him, is only preparing trouble for himself. Sometimes it is wiser to overlook altogether the remarks made upon us, sometimes to laugh at them. Socrates, on receiving a slap in the face, merely said, 'What a pity it is that one does not know when to put a helmet on before going out.' On another occasion, when his friends expressed astonishment, because having been kicked by an unmannerly lout, he patiently put up with the outrage, he said, 'Why not, if an ass had lifted his heels against me, do you think I should have taken out a summons against him?' Again, when he was told that so and so was always abusing him, he merely replied, 'Ah, he never learnt good manners.'

232. In this person were collected the most opposite defects and advantages of every kind. He was avaricious and ostentatious, despotic and obliging, politic and confiding, licentious and superstitious, bold and timid, ambitious and indiscreet; lavish of his bounty to his relations, his mistresses and his favourites; yet frequently paying neither his household nor his creditors. His consequence always depended on a woman, and he was always unfaithful to her. Nothing could equal the activity of his mind, nor the indolence of his body. No dangers could appal his courage, no difficulties force him to abandon his projects. But the success of an enterprise always brought on disgust. Everything with him was desultory; business, pleasure, temper, courage. His presence was a restraint on every company. He was morose to all that stood in awe of him, and caressed all such as accosted him with familiarity. Banished by his rival, he ran to meet death in battle, and returned with glory.

Tacitus, *Hist.* i. 10, 49; ii. 5.
Sallust, *Catil.* 5, 23.
Cornelius Nepos, *Alcibiades*, i. 11.

233. His natural endowments were great for any part in public life, whether at the bar, or in the senate, or even in war; for the part of a revolutionary leader they were of the highest order. A courage which nothing could quell; a quickness of perception at once and clearly to perceive his own opportunity, and his adversary's error; singular fertility of resources, with the power of sudden change in his course, and adaptation to varied circumstances; a natural eloquence, hardy, caustic, masculine; a mighty frame of body, a voice overpowering all resistance;—these were the grand qualities which Danton brought to the prodigious struggle in which he was engaged.

Livy, xxii. 25, 26; xxxix. 40.   Sallust, *Catil.* 1, 5.

234. In person the prince was tall and well-formed: his limbs athletic and active. He excelled in all manly exercises, and was inured to every kind of toil, especially long marches on foot, having applied himself to field sports in Italy, and become an excellent walker. His face was strikingly handsome, of a perfect oval, and a fair complexion; his eyes light blue; his features high and noble. Contrary to the custom of the time, he wore his own hair long and falling in ringlets on his neck. This goodly person was enhanced by his graceful manners; frequently condescending to the most familiar kindness, yet always shielded by a regal dignity, he had a peculiar talent to please and to persuade, and never failed to adapt his conversation to the taste or to the station of those whom he addressed.

Suetonius, *Octavian*, 79.   *J. Cæsar*, 45.   Livy, xxviii. 35.

235. He was not without a certain aptitude for military pursuits, and possessed considerable courage. But so crack-brained and eccentric was he in his general conduct and behaviour, that he came before long to be called 'the Madman.' For instance, he used frequently to sally out from the palace without the knowledge of his ministers, with a single companion or so, and stroll through the streets, with a wreath of flowers on his head, and wearing a gold embroidered doublet, and pelt the people he met with stones which he used to carry under his arm. Sometimes again, he would scatter money among the rabble, crying out, 'catch who can.' At other times he would visit the goldsmith's and picture-dealer's shops, and talk learnedly about 'Art,' and at others, stop and talk in the middle of the street with the first comer, or make a round of the taverns, and indulge in a carouse with tramps and scamps of the lowest sort.

236. His resolution was immediately formed : he rose and called together the officers of the Greeks and addressed them. After having pointed out the magnitude of the evils which they had to apprehend, unless some provision were made without delay for their defence, he dexterously turned their attention to a more animating view of the situation. Ever since they had concluded the treaty with Tissaphernes, he had observed with envy and regret the rich possessions of the barbarians, and had lamented that his comrades had bound themselves to abstain from the good things which they saw within their reach, except so far as they were able to purchase a taste of them at an expense which he had feared would soon exhaust their scanty means.

237. They had crossed the plain to the foot of the hills in the dark, during the last watch of the night, and found the passes unguarded. But the people fled from the villages at their approach, and though the Greeks at first spared their property, could not be induced to listen to any pacific overtures. But having recovered from their first surprise, and collected a part of their forces, they fell upon the rear of the Greeks, and with their missiles made some slaughter among the last troops which issued in the dusk of the evening from the long and narrow defile. In the night the watch-fires of the Carduchians were seen blazing on the peaks of the surrounding hills : signals which warned the Greeks that they might expect to be attacked by the collected forces of their tribes.

238. On the fifth day, as the army was ascending

mount Theche, a lofty ridge distinguished by the name of the Sacred Mountain, Xenophon and the rear guard observed a stoppage and an unusual clamour in the foremost ranks, which had reached the summit, and they supposed at first that they saw an enemy before them. But when Xenophon rode up to ascertain the cause, the first shouts that struck his ear were, *The sea, the sea!* The glad sound ran quickly till it reached the hindmost, and all pressed forward to enjoy the cheering spectacle. The Euxine spread its waters before their eyes; waters which rolled on to the shores of Greece, and which washed the walls of many Greek cities on the nearest coast of Asia.

239. While the two armies fronted each other, and were on the very eve of battle, a hind came running down from the mountains between the two opposing lines, with a wolf in chase of her. She ran in among the Gaulish ranks, and the Gauls transfixed her with their long javelins. The wolf ran towards the Romans, and they instantly gave free passage to the beast which had given suck to the founder of their city, and whose image they had only in the preceding year set up beneath that very sacred fig-tree in the comitium, which tradition pointed out as the scene of the miracle. 'See,' cried out one of the soldiers, 'Diana's sacred hind has been slain by the barbarians, and will bring down her wrath upon them: while the Roman wolf, unhurt by sword or spear, gives us a fair omen of victory, and bids us think on Mars and on Quirinus our divine founder.' So the Roman soldiers, as if encouraged by a sign from the gods, rushed cheerfully to the onset.

240. Pizarro, when the messengers reported there was no water to be found, at last bade the skin carriers follow him down to the sea, which was less than 300 yards distant, and dig in different places a little way from each other. A mountain range not far off gave him hopes of finding water, for seeing they had no surface streams running from them, he made sure that they contained hidden springs, which percolating by channels underground must find their way to the sea. Scarcely was an opening made in the ground, before streams of water, muddy at first and of slender volume, gushed out, and presently a clear and abundant flow, the gift as it were of providence. This circumstance increased not a little the faith of the soldiers in their general. He then ordered the soldiers to get their arms ready: while he himself, accompanied by his officers and a small escort, went on to explore the pass, and to find out where they could the most easily descend with their armour on, and where the ascent was least precipitous on the other side.

241. One day Piso in a rage ordered a soldier to be led to execution, on a charge of having murdered a comrade, in whose company he had gone out of camp, but had returned without him. The man asked for time to have enquiries made, but Piso refused. The doomed soldier was taken outside the rampart, and was preparing to receive the fatal stroke, when suddenly his comrade appeared, whom he was said to have killed. Then the officer, who had charge of the execution, bade the executioner put up his sword: the two soldiers embraced each other; and then followed by a large crowd, with much rejoicing, they were escorted to Piso's quarters. But he mounted the judgment seat in a furious passion, and ordered them both to be put to death : and with them the officer who had brought back the condemned man, with these words, 'I order you to be punished with death, because you have been already condemned : you, because you have been the cause of your comrades' sentence : and you, because you disobeyed your general, when ordered to carry the sentence into execution.'

242. At last his caprice took the form of fancying himself a Roman. Substituting for his royal robes a toga, as he had seen candidates for office do at Rome ; he walked about the forum shaking hands with and embracing individual citizens, and canvassing their votes at one time for the aedileship, at another for a tribuneship of the people. Then pretending to have been elected, he caused an ivory chair to be set for him, from which he gave judgment, summing up the pros and cons in some imaginary case. And so fickle and flighty was he, now fancying himself one thing, now another, that his real nature became a matter of uncertainty to himself as well as those about him. Sometimes he would refuse to speak to his friends, or to nod to his acquaintances. He made himself and others ridiculous by unsuitable presents : giving to certain highly respectable friends, people who stood upon their dignity, sweetmeats and toys. And so it was concluded by some that his majesty did not know what he was doing, while others said he was mad, others that he was only joking.

243. Towards the close of his reign his conduct be-

came more intolerable, and at last he took care to advertise all Europe of his folly or madness, or both, by inserting in the St. Petersburgh Gazette a notice to the following effect, 'That the Emperor of Russia, finding the powers of Europe cannot agree among themselves, and being desirous to put an end to a war, which has desolated it for eleven years, intends to point out a spot to which he will invite all the other sovereigns to repair and fight in single combat, bringing with them as seconds and esquires, their most enlightened ministers and able generals, and that the Emperor himself proposes being attended by generals Count Pahlen and Kutusoff.' This piece of extravagance appears to have completed the disgust of the nobles and to have consummated his ruin.

244. When they arrived at Westminster, he being unable to walk on account of his age, and being carried in a sedan, a great concourse was assembled. And some remembering his former glory pitied the old man, but the greater part were filled with anger against him, on account of his supposed betrayal of the port, but chiefly because he had thwarted the interests of the populace in his later years, on which charge he had not even been allowed the opportunity of defending himself and of pleading his own cause. So after certain legal formalities had been gone through, he was condemned and handed over to the executioner. When he was being led to death, a Mr. Goodlove, whom he had known intimately, met him, and with tears exclaimed, 'Alack, then, Sir John! how unjustly you are treated, how undeserved are your sufferings!' 'But not unexpected,'

he replied, 'this is the end that most good men have
met with in our country !'

Cicero, *Tusc. Quæst.* i. 96 sqq.

245. After this ceremony he was delivered to the
secular power.   His last interview with his family is thus
simply told.   Now when the Sheriffe and his company
came against St. Botolph Church, Elisabeth cried, saying,
'O my deare Father! Mother, Mother, is my father led
away?'   Then cried his wife, 'Rowland, Rowland, where
art thou?' for it was a verie darke morning, that the one
could not see the other.   Dr. Taylor answered, 'Deare
wife, I am here,' and staid.   The Sheriffes men would
have led him forth, but the Sheriffe said, 'Stay a little,
maisters, I praie you, and let him speake to his wife,'
and so they staid.

246. Then came she to him, and he tooke his daughter
Mary in his armes, and he, his wife, and Elisabeth,
kneeled down and said the Lord's Praier; at which sight
the Sheriffe wept apace, and so did divers other of the
company.   After they had praied, he rose up and kissed
his wife, and tooke her by the hand, and said, 'Farewell,
my deare wife, bee of good comfort, for I am quiet in
my conscience.   God shall stir up a father for my
children.'   And then he kissed his daughter Mary, and
said, 'God blesse thee, and make thee his servant.'
And kissing Elisabeth, he said, 'God blesse thee, I pray
you all stand strong and steadfast unto Christ and his
worde, and keep you from idolatry.'   Then said his wife,
'God be with thee, dear Rowland.   I will, with God's
grace, meet thee at Hadley.'

247. When they had all drunk to him, and the cup was come to him, he stayed a little, as one studying what answer he might give. At the last, thus he answered, and said, ' Master Sheriffe, and my masters all, I heartily thank you for your good will; I have hearkened to your words, and marked well your counsels; and to be plaine with you, I do perceive that I have been deceived myself, and am likely to deceive a great many of Hadley of their expectation.' With that word they all rejoiced. 'Yes, good Master Doctor,' quoth the Sheriffe, 'God's blessing on your heart, hold you there still. It is the comfortablest word that we heard you speak yet. What, should ye cast yourself away in vain? Play a wise man's part, and I dare warrant it, ye shall find favour.' Thus they rejoiced very much at the word, and were very merry.

Cicero, *Tusc. Quæst.* i. § 96 sqq., 103 sqq.

248. At the last, 'Good Master Doctor,' quoth the Sheriffe, 'what meane ye by this, that ye said ye think ye have been deceived yourselfe, and think ye shall deceive many one in Hadley?' 'Would ye know my meaning plainly?' quoth he. 'Yes,' quoth the Sheriffe, 'good Master Doctor, tell it us plainly.' 'Then,' said Dr. Taylor, 'I will tell you how I have been deceived, and, as I think, I shall deceive a great many more. I am, as you see, a man that hath a very great carkasse, which I thought should have been buried in Hadley churchyard, if I had died in my bed, as I well hoped I should have done : but herein I see I was deceived ; and there are a great number of wormes in Hadley churchyard, which should have had jolly feeding on this carrion; which they have looked for many a day. But now I know we be deceived, both I and they. For this carkasse must be burnt to ashes, and so shall they lose their bait and feeding, that they looked to have had of it.'

Cicero, *Tusc. Quæst.* i. § 103, 104.

249. On the 5th of February he was brought out to complete his earthly journey. The same spirit animated him to the end. On the way, being alighted from his horse, he lept and fet a friske or twaine, as men commonly do in daucing. 'Why, Master Doctor,' quoth the Sheriffe, 'how do you now?' He answered, 'Well, God be praised, never better, for now I know I am almost at home. I lack not past two stiles to go over, and I am even at my father's house.' At last, coming to Aldham Common, the place assigned where he should suffer, and seeing a great multitude of people gathered together, he asked, 'What place is this, and what meaneth it that so much people are gathered hither?' It was answered, 'It is Aldham Common, the place where you must suffer; and the people are come to looke upon you.' 'Then,' said he, 'thanked be God, I am even at home.' And so light from his horse. As they were piling the faggots, one Warwick cruelly cast a faggot at him, which light on his head, and broke his face, that the bloud ran down his visage. Then said Doctor Taylor, 'O friend, I have harme enough; what needed that?'

250. There was at Athens a large roomy house. But the house had a bad name, people shunned it as if plague-stricken. Noises were heard there in the silence of night, and if you listened you could hear the clanking of chains, beginning some way off and then coming nearer.   And then a ghost used to appear in the likeness of an old man squalid and worn, with a long beard and unkempt hair.   On his legs were fetters, and chains on his hands, which rattled as he moved.   The occupants used to spend whole nights lying awake in an agony of terror.   They fell sick, and death followed their ex- cessive fright.   For even in the day time, although the apparition was no longer visible, the memory of it haunted them : and the fear still oppressed them when the cause was removed.   The house in consequence was deserted, given up entirely to the ghost ; although it continued to be advertised 'to be let, or sold,' on the chance of a stranger taking it.

251. There came to Athens one Athenodorus, a philo- sopher.   He read the notice, and ascertained the price, but his suspicions being aroused by the cheapness, he made inquiries, was told the whole story, and determined in spite of all to take the house.   As soon as evening drew on, he ordered a desk and chair to be set for him in a front room ; and had his note-book brought, with pens and ink and a light.   He then dismissed his attendants, and set himself to write, concentrating all his faculties on the task, that his mind might not wander and conjure up imaginary sights and terrors.   At first a dead silence prevailed, then came a clanging of iron, and a rattling of chains.   However, he would not lift his eyes, nor stop writing, determined to keep his thoughts fixed and his ears shut.   The noise grew louder and seemed to come nearer, now it was at the door, now in the room itself.   He looked over his shoulder, and there he saw the ghost, just as it had been described to him.

252. The figure stood and beckoned with its finger, as if to summon him : the philosopher in reply motioned with his hand, as if bidding the ghost to wait a little, and again bent down to his writing.   Then the apparition shook its chains over the head of the writing man, who once more looked up, and seeing the beckoning repeated, got up at once, took the light and followed.   The form moved slowly on as if retarded by the weight of its chains; then turning into the court-yard, suddenly vanished.   The philosopher, finding himself alone, gathered some grass and leaves and laid them down to mark the spot.   That day he goes to the magistrate, and requests him to send and have a hole dug at the place.   And what do you think?   There they found a skeleton, with a chain wound about it.   The flesh decayed with time and decomposed had fallen away and left the bones bare and rust-eaten.   The remains were collected, and publicly buried.   So the ghost was duly laid, and the house was haunted no more.

253. Meanwhile the Vestal virgins, taking no care about their own property, first settled among themselves which of the holy vessels should be taken with them and which left, because they were not strong enough to carry them all; they then buried a part within the precincts, enclosed in jars; and carrying the rest, having divided the burdens, they took the road which led to the Janiculum. On the way they were espied by one Albinus, a poor man, who was conveying his wife and children in a waggon, among the rest of the population then crowding out of the city. He thought it wicked that the holy sisters should be walking on foot, carrying in their hands the precious relics, while he and his were riding in a waggon. Therefore, postponing his own journey, he told his wife and children to get down, and then placing the Vestals and their sacred utensils in the waggon, he drove them to Cære, the place they were bound for.

254. The approach of night, though it delivered the dejected Spaniards from the attacks of the enemy, ushered in, what was hardly less grievous, the noise of their barbarous triumph, and of the horrid festival with which they celebrated their victory. Every quarter of the city was illuminated; the great temple shone with such peculiar splendour, that the Spaniards could plainly see the people in motion, and the priests busy in hastening preparations for the death of the prisoners. Through the gloom they fancied that they discerned their companions by the whiteness of their skins, as they were stript naked, and compelled to dance before the image of the god to whom they were to be offered. They heard the shrieks of those who were sacrificed, and thought that they could distinguish each unhappy victim, by the well-known sound of his voice.

Livy, x. 38.

255. Menenius Agrippa, surnamed Lanatus, was chosen general against the Sabines, and triumphed over them. And when the populace had seceded from the Senate, because they could not endure the tribute and military service laid upon them, and when it was found impossible to recall them, Agrippa told them the following story: 'Once upon a time, the human limbs, seeing the belly idle, quarrelled with it, and refused their services. When by that means they too lost their strength, they understood that the belly dispersed over all the limbs the food that it received, and became reconciled to it. Even so the Senate and people made up, as it were, one body, of which concord is the strength, and discord the destruction.'

Livy, ii. 32.

256. 'I am come to inform you of a secret you must impart to Pausanias alone. From remote antiquity I am of Grecian lineage. I am solicitous of the safety of Greece. Long since, but for the auguries, would Mardonius have given battle. Regarding these no longer, he will attack you early in the morning. Be prepared. If he change his purpose, remain as you are—he has provisions only for a few days more. Should the event of war prove favourable, you will but deem it fitting to make some effort for the independence of one who exposes himself to so great a peril for the purpose of apprising you of the intentions of the foe. I am Alexander of Macedon.'

257. We were a little uneasy, however, when we found it snowed one whole day and a night, so fast, that we could not travel; but the guide bid us be easy, we should soon be past it all; and so we struggled on. It was about two hours before night, when our guide being something before us, and not just in sight, out rushed three monstrous wolves, from the thick wood adjoining.

Two of the wolves flew upon the guide, and had he been half a mile before us, he had been devoured before we could have helped him. One of them fastened upon his horse, and the other attacked the man with that violence, that he had not time, or not presence of mind enough, to draw his weapon, but hallooed to us most lustily. My man Friday being next to me, I bad him ride up and see what was the matter.

258. 'These are the mansions of good men after death, who, according to the degree and kinds of virtue in which they excelled, are distributed among these several islands ; which abound with pleasures of different kinds and degrees, suitable to the relishes and perfections of those who are settled in them : every island is a paradise accommodated to its respective inhabitants. Are not these, O Mirza, habitations worth contending for? Does life appear miserable that gives thee opportunities of earning such a reward? Is death to be feared that will convey thee to so happy an existence? Think not man was made in vain who has such an eternity reserved for him.' I gazed with inexpressible pleasure on these happy islands. At length said I, 'Shew me now, I beseech thee, the secrets that lie hid under those dark clouds which cover the ocean on the other side of the rock of adamant.' The genius making me no answer, I turned about to address myself to him a second time, but I found that he had left me.

259. One Dicæus, an Athenian exile in the Persian service, asserted that one day, when he was in the Thriasian plain, which stretches from Eleusis north-

L

ward, in company with Demaratus, the banished king of Sparta, who followed in Xerxes' train, they saw a cloud of dust, such as might be raised by the trampling of many thousand men, advance from Eleusis. As they were wondering what this might be, they heard a noise which seemed to him to be the song which the initiated sang in praise of Iacchus. Dicæus then assured his companion that some great evil was about to befal the Persians : for the gods were manifestly quitting Eleusis, on the desolation of Attica, to proceed .to the assistance of the Greeks, and if they should direct their course towards Peloponnesus, the blow would fall on the land army: if towards Salamis, then Xerxes would run great risk of losing his fleet.

Cicero, de Divinat. i. 44. § 100.

260. Philip of Macedon had a soldier of great personal courage, whose assistance he had often found valuable in his expeditions, and whose bravery he had in consequence frequently rewarded by grants from the treasury, till by re-peated acts of bounty he had roused the spirit of avarice in his heart. This fellow was wrecked and cast ashore on the estate of a certain Macedonian, who, as soon as he heard of it, ran up, recovered him from his swoon, carried him to his own house, gave up his own bed to him, and, suffering and half dead as he was, made a new man of him, entertained him for thirty days at his own cost, and furnished him with provision for the journey, so that he exclaimed at parting, 'Let me only have the luck to catch sight of my general, and your kindness shall not go unrewarded.'

261. Well, he reaches home, gives Philip an account

of his shipwreck, says nothing about the help which had been given him, but proceeds to ask him for the grant of a certain person's farm. Now, that person was none other than the very man who had entertained him, taken him in, and restored him to health. But kings, especially when occupied in wars, have to make many grants blindfold; for how else will so many thousands have their inordinate cravings satisfied, or how be benefited, if every one is merely to have his own? So soliloquized Philip, as he gave orders for the fellow to be put in possession of the coveted estate.

Cicero, *de Officiis*, iii. 14.

262. At the city-gate they separated. A strange slave had followed them at a distance all the way. He now stood still for a moment, apparently undetermined which of the two he should pursue. ' Youth is more liberal,' said he half aloud, after reflecting a moment, 'especially when in love.' With this he struck into the path Charicles had taken, and which led through a narrow lonely lane between two garden-walls; here he redoubled his pace and soon overtook Charicles. 'Who art thou?' asked the youth, retreating back a step. ' A slave, as you see,' was the reply, 'and one who may be of service to you. You seem interested in Cleobule's fate, eh?' ' What business is that of yours?' retorted Charicles; but his blush was more than a sufficient answer for the slave. ' It is not indifferent to you,' he proceeded, ' whether Sophilos or Sosilas be the heir.' 'Very possibly; but wherefore these enquiries? What is this to you, sirrah?' ' More than you think,' rejoined the slave.

263. Pompey sailed to Cilicia, the seat and birthplace of the rebellion. The enemy made but a faint show of resistance, collapsing under the first blow. For as soon as they saw his ships bearing down upon them on all sides, they immediately threw down their arms, and ceased rowing, and with a general clapping of hands, which was their way of asking quarter, begged that their lives might be spared. Never did we gain so bloodless a victory: and never did a people prove more faithful to us after their defeat. This was due to the singular foresight and judgment of Pompey, who caused the seafaring population to be transplanted from the sea-board, and kept in the inland districts. Thus he at the same time rendered the sea open to commerce, and supplied the land with cultivators. One hardly knows which to admire most in this campaign : the swiftness with which ·it was conducted, it was finished in forty days ; the good fortune that attended it, not a single ship was lost ; or the permanence of its effects ; there were never any more pirates.

264. The horsemen rode off in anger, and the sailors again changing their minds, came to land, and casting anchor at the mouth of the Liris, which spreads out like a lake, they advised Marius to disembark, and take some food on land, and to rest himself from his fatigues till a wind should rise : they added, that it was the usual time for the sea-breeze to decline, and for a fresh breeze to spring up from the marshes. Marius did as they advised, and the sailors carried him out of the vessel, and laid him on the grass little expecting what was to follow. The sailors immediately embarking again, and raising the anchor, sailed off as fast as they could, not thinking it honourable to surrender Marius, or safe to protect him.

265. In this situation, deserted by everybody, he lay for some time silent on the shore, and at last, recovering himself with difficulty, he walked on with much pain on account of there being no path. After passing through deep swamps and ditches full of water and mud, he came to the hut of an old man who worked in the marshes, and falling down at his feet, besought him to save and help a man who, if he escaped from the present dangers, would reward him beyond all his hopes. The man, who either knew Marius of old, or saw something in the ex-pression of his countenance which denoted superior rank, said that his hut was sufficient to shelter him if that was all he wanted, but if he was wandering about to avoid his enemies, he could conceal him in a place that was more retired. Upon Marius entreating him to do so, the old man took him to the marsh, and bidding him lie down in a hole near the river, covered Marius with reeds and other light things, which were well adapted to hide him without pressing too heavily.

266. After a short time a sound and noise from the hut reached the ears of Marius. Geminius of Terracina had sent a number of men in pursuit of him, some of whom had chanced to come there, and were terrifying the old man and rating him for having harboured and concealed an enemy of the Romans. Marius, rising from his hiding-place, and stripping off his clothes, threw him-self into the thick and muddy water of the marsh; and this was the cause of his not escaping the search of his pursuers, who dragged him out covered with mud, and leading him naked to Minturnæ, gave him to the magistrates. Now instructions had been already sent to every city requiring the authorities to search for Marius, and to put him to death when he was taken.

267. The magistrates and council of Minturnæ, after deliberating, resolved that there ought to be no delay, and that they should put Marius to death. As none of the citizens would undertake to do it, a Gallic or Cimbrian horse-soldier (for the story is told both ways) took a sword and entered the apartment. Now that part of the room in which Marius happened to be lying was not very well lighted, but was in shade, and it is said that the eyes of Marius appeared to the soldier to dart a strong flame, and a loud voice issued from the gloom —'Man, do you dare to kill Caius Marius?' The barbarian immediately took to flight, and throwing the sword down, rushed through the door, calling out, 'I cannot kill Caius Marius.' This caused a general consternation, which was succeeded by compassion and change of opinion, and self-reproach, for having resolved to hurt a man who had saved Italy, and whom it would be a disgrace not to assist.

268. When the Athenians were informed that the troops who were at Pylos had not yet captured the Lacedæmonians, and that their hopes were failing, they did not know what to do. And Cleon, fearing lest they should be angry with him, because he had prevented them from making peace before, said that the messengers had not spoken truly. And since he was an enemy of Nicias, he cast blame also upon the generals; 'for,' said he, 'if the generals had been *men*, they would have taken it long ago; and if I were elected, I could easily finish the war.' Hereupon Nicias replied that he had better go there, if he thought it so easy, and he would give him his general's command. At this Cleon was astounded, and tried to change what he had said, since he did not expect that Nicias would resign his command. But the people were not sorry when the boastful Cleon was caught in his own snare, and though he was unwilling to go, so much the more they urged him to do as he had said.

269. They say that Lucius Manlius was a very successful general. He was, however, cruel to his soldiers, and crueller still to his son. For the youth, as he had always lacked good teaching, was awkward in appearance and speech. This circumstance so annoyed Manlius that he would not suffer his innocent son to remain at home, but drove him from the society of his equals to labour among slaves in the fields. On hearing this, the tribune of the Plebs, whose duty it was to aid the oppressed, issued a summons against the cruel parent. It seemed, however, better to the youth to undergo any hardship than to be the cause of disgrace and ruin to his father. Accordingly he went to the tribune's house at daybreak, and burst into the chamber where the owner was then sleeping. First he explained who he was, then, drawing a sword, he declared that he would kill the tribune if he persisted in the matter. 'Promise,' said he, 'that you will not accuse my father, or

I will slay you on the spot!' The tribune, greatly alarmed, dared not resist, and obeyed the young man's demand. Thus the virtue of a dutiful son saved this unnatural father from well-deserved punishment.

Livy, vii. 5.   Seneca, *de Beneficiis*, iii. 37.

270. Then was committed that great crime, memorable for its singular atrocity, memorable for the tremendous retribution that followed it. The English captives were left to the mercy of the guards, and the guards determined to secure them for the night in the prison of the garrison, a chamber known by the fearful name of the Black Hole. Even for a single European malefactor, that dungeon would in such a climate have been too close and narrow. The space was only twenty feet square; the air-holes small and obstructed. It was the summer solstice, the season when the fierce heat of Bengal can scarcely be rendered tolerable to natives of England by lofty halls and by the constant waving of fans. The number of the prisoners was one hundred and forty-six.

271. When they were ordered to enter the cell, they imagined that the soldiers were joking; and being in high spirits on account of the promise of the Nabob to spare their lives, they laughed and jested at the absurdity of the notion. They soon discovered their mistake. They expostulated, they entreated, but in vain. The guards threatened to cut down all who hesitated. The captives were driven into the cell at the point of the sword, and the door was instantly shut and locked upon them. Nothing in history or fiction approaches the horrors which were recounted by the few survivors of that night.

They cried for mercy. They strove to burst the door. Holwell, who even in that extremity retained some presence of mind, offered large bribes to the gaolers. But the answer was, that nothing could be done without the Nabob's orders, that the Nabob was asleep, and that he would be angry if anybody woke him.

272. Then the prisoners went mad with despair. They trampled each other down, fought for the places at the windows, fought for the pittance of water with which the cruel mercy of the murderers mocked their agonies, raved, prayed, blasphemed, implored the guards to fire among them. The gaolers in the meantime held lights to the bars, and shouted with laughter at the frantic struggles of their victims. At length the tumult died away in low gaspings and moanings. The day broke. The Nabob had slept off his debauch, and permitted the door to be opened. But it was some time before the soldiers could make a lane for the survivors, by piling up on each side the heaps of corpses on which the burning climate had already begun to do its loathsome work.

273. We may compare the career of Rome with the life of a man. In reviewing its whole history, how it began, how it grew up, and reached the fulness of manhood, and then fell into decay, we shall find four periods of development. The first stage was under the kings, lasting about two hundred and fifty years, which it passed near the cradle of the race in struggling with the neighbouring communities. This may be called the infancy of Rome. The next period extends over two hundred and fifty years, from the consulship of Brutus and

Collatinus, to that of Appius Claudius and Q. Fulvius, during which it subdued Italy. This was the most stirring period, and may be called the youth of Rome. From that time to the reign of Augustus, was two hundred years, during which Rome brought the whole world into subjection. This was the age of its manhood, and the maturity of its power. From that time forward Rome gradually declined; yet in its old age, it shewed an unexpected renewal of vigour, under the beneficent sway of Trajan.

274. Nature gave you, my friend, the heart of a king, but she gave you not a kingdom, of which therefore Fortune could not deprive you. But I doubt whether our age can furnish an example of worse or better treatment from her than yourself. In the first part of your life you were blest with an admirable constitution, and astonishing health and vigour : some years after we beheld you thrice abandoned by the physicians who despaired of your life. The heavenly Physician, who was your sole resource, restored you to health, but not to your former strength. You were then called iron-footed, for your singular force and agility : you are now bent, and lean upon the shoulders of those whom you formerly supported. Your country beheld you one day its governor, the next an exile.

Seneca, de Consolatione ad Polyb. 25.

275. Princes disputed for your friendship, and afterwards conspired your ruin. You lost by death the greatest part of your friends : the rest, according to custom, deserted you in calamity. To these misfortunes was added a violent disease, which attacked you when destitute of all succours, at a distance from your country and family, in a strange land, invested by the troops of your enemies : so that those two or three friends, whom fortune had left you, could not come near to relieve you. In a word, you have experienced every hardship but imprisonment and death. But what do I say ? You have felt all the horrors of the former, when your faithful wife and children were shut up by your enemies : and even death followed you, and took one of those children, for whose life you would willingly have sacrificed your own.

Seneca, *de Consolatione ad Polyb.* 25.

276. I said, there was a society of men among us, bred up from their youth, in the art of proving, by words multiplied for the purpose, that white is black, and black is white, according as they are paid. To this society, all the rest of the people are slaves. For example, if my neighbour hath a mind to my cow, he hires a lawyer to prove that he ought to have my cow from me. I must then hire another to defend my right : it being against all rules of law, that any man should be allowed to speak for himself. Now, in this case, I, who am the right owner, lie under two great disadvantages ; first, my lawyer, being practised almost from his cradle, in defending falsehood, is quite out of his element, when he will be an advocate for justice.

Cicero, *pro Murena,* 12.

277. Meanwhile a certain Gaul, armed only with a shield and a sword, and decorated with a collar and armlets, stepped forth. He was a gigantic warrior, surpassing all the rest both in strength and courage. So in the heat of the battle, when both sides were fighting with the utmost fury, he began waving his hands as a sign to the combatants to stop fighting. A pause followed. Then, in the midst of a deep silence, he proclaimed in a loud voice, 'If any one is willing to fight with me, let him come forth.' But no one dared, such was his bigness and the fierceness of his look. Thereupon the Gaul began to gibe and make faces. This was too much for T. Manlius, a young Roman of noble birth. It pained him that such dishonour should befal his country, and that no one out of so great a host should stand forth to fight the Gaul. So out he stepped himself, and suffered not foul scorn to be cast upon the valour of the Romans: but armed with a buckler and a Spanish sword, he took his stand opposite the foe.

Livy, vii. 9.

278. The meeting took place near the approach to the bridge, while both armies looked on in breathless expectation. They took their places then, as I said before. The Gaul, as he had been trained to do, sheltered himself behind his shield, and waited. Manlius, trusting to valour rather than to skill, dashed his own shield against the shield of the other, and threw the Gaul off his balance. Then, while the Gaul is trying to recover himself and resume his position, Manlius makes a second dash at him with his shield, and a second time dislodges him from his posture of defence. Seizing his advantage, he forced himself under his adversary's guard, so that the Gaul could not gather force for a stroke, and drawing his

dagger plunged it into the other's breast, and, following
up the blow, pressed with all his might against his
enemy's right shoulder, and never relaxed his effort until
he had thrown him over. When he had fallen Manlius
cut his head off, drew the collar from him, and put it, all
bloody as it was, upon his own neck. From which
exploit both he and his descendants were surnamed
Torquati.

Livy, vii. 9.

279. At a seaport to the westward of this city lived,
some time since, a merchant who by numerous voyages
had acquired a large fortune, and who preserving a taste
for his early profession, frequently amused himself during
the summer by sailing from island to island. He had an
only son to whom he had given an excellent education,
and the young man though only fifteen years old, had so
far penetrated into the most difficult secrets of nature as
to have acquired the language of birds. One day while
the father and son were sailing in a new and favourite
vessel, a pair of ravens continued for some time to flutter
over their heads, occasionally settling on the mast or in
the shrouds, and croaking so incessantly that the old
merchant was much disturbed, and almost deafened by
their noise. 'I wish,' cried he, 'since I cannot silence
those vile birds, that I could at least discover the subject
of their discourse !'

280. 'Their discourse,' replied the son, 'is addressed
to me; they have been telling my fortune; and they
assure me that I shall one day be much richer and more
powerful than thou art, and that a time will come when

thou shalt be happy to support the sleeve of my cloak whilst I am washing : and that my mother will be proud of holding the towel to wipe my hands.' ' Indeed !' exclaimed the father, ' art thou so discontented and ambitious?   But I will soon try whether the croakers are not mistaken in their prophecy !'   With these words he suddenly caught the youth round the waist, and threw him headlong into the sea : after which he altered his course, and still boiling with indignation, sailed back to port. The youth was fortunately an expert swimmer, and seeing an island at some distance, succeeded at length by the help of Providence, in reaching the shore.

281. And it was now near the setting of the sun ; for he had been away in the inner room for a long time. But when he came in from bathing he sat down and did not speak much afterwards ; for then the servant of the Eleven came in, and standing near him, said, ' I do not perceive that in you, Socrates, which I have taken notice of in others : I mean, that they are angry with me and curse me, when being compelled by the magistrates I announce to them that they must drink the poison. But on the contrary, I have found you to the present time to be the most generous, mild, and best of all the men that ever came into this place ; and therefore I am well convinced that you are not angry with me, but with the authors of your present condition, for you know who they are.   Now therefore, for you know what I came to tell you, farewell ; and endeavour to bear this necessity as easily as possible.'

282. Then Criton, hearing this, gave a sign to the boy

that stood near him ; and the boy departing, and having stayed for some time, came back with the person that was to administer the poison, who brought it pounded in a cup. And Socrates, looking at the man, said, ' Well, my friend, as you are knowing in these matters, what is to be done ?' ' Nothing,' he said, ' but after you have drunk it to walk about, until a heaviness comes on in your legs, and then to lie down : this is the manner in which you have to act.' And at the same time he extended the cup to Socrates. And Socrates taking it—and, indeed, with great cheerfulness, neither trembling nor turning colour, but as his manner was, looking sternly under his brows at the man—' What say you,' he said, ' to making a libation from this ? may I do it or not ?'

283. The Roman general obtained possession of the enemy's camp, and abandoned all the booty to the soldiery : such prisoners as were of Spanish origin he suffered to go home without a ransom, but ordered the Africans to be sold into slavery. Amongst these was a youth of royal birth, and of such remarkable beauty that the general stopped and enquired of him who he was and how he happened to be serving in the army at that age. In reply the boy said he was a Numidian, and that his countrymen called him Massiva. He had been left an orphan, he said, by the death of his father, and had crossed over into Spain with his uncle Masinissa, who had lately come to help the Carthaginians, and by reason of his youth had never been allowed to take part in an engagement. On the day of the encounter with the Romans he had secretly taken a horse and armour and gone out to fight without his uncle's knowledge ; but owing to his horse's stumbling, had been thrown down and taken prisoner by the enemy. Hereupon Scipio asked him if he would like to go back to his uncle. The boy, shedding tears of delight, said that he certainly would. So the Roman made him a present of a gold ring and a richly caparisoned horse, and, giving him an escort of cavalry to conduct him, let him go free and unharmed.

284. They sent deputies to the Roman general, offering him his choice of peace or war. It was the custom, they said, of their nation never to decline the combat with an enemy who challenged them : however they had gained their immediate object ; they had found the settlements they sought ; with the Romans they had no quarrel ; they were content to remain upon the soil they had seized. They boasted the valour by which these acquisitions had been so rapidly made, and ended by declaring that they yielded in strength and bravery to no nation, excepting only the Suevi, whom the gods themselves could not withstand. Cæsar replied, as was his wont, that it was the duty of a Roman proconsul to protect the Gauls against all external enemies. He would hold no intercourse or discussion with any foreign nation, while it occupied an inch of Gallic soil.

Cæsar, *de Bello Gallico*, i. 13.

285. The route by which the army was marching led across the fatal field. As they traversed the high plain of Calaluz the soldiers saw everywhere around the traces of the fight. The ground was still covered with fragments of armour, with broken swords and spears, and a still sadder sight were the bones of men and horses, which in this solitary region had been whitening in the blasts of seventy winters. Here was the spot where the vanguard had halted in the obscurity of the night. There were the remains of the enemy's entrenchments which time had nearly levelled with the dust ; and there, too, the rocks still threw their dark shadows over the plain, as on the day when the valiant Alonso fell fighting at their base. The whole battle handed down from the lips of their fathers came back to the memory of the Spaniards, and as they gazed on the unburied relics lying around them, the tears fell fast from their iron cheeks.

Tacitus, Ann. i. 61.

286. When Cyrus was twelve years old he went with his mother to visit Astyages, who desired to see him because he heard that he was beautiful and of a noble disposition. At dinner, Astyages used to order the best dishes of all kinds to be set before the boy, who had not been accustomed to such magnificence. Once when Cyrus saw a great quantity of food set before him he asked whether he might dispose of it according to his pleasure ; and being told that he might, he proceeded to distribute it to the attendants—all except Sacas, the king's cup-bearer. Then Astyages asked why he gave Sacas nothing. And Cyrus said, ' Because there is poison in the wine which he gives you, and this I perceived the other day when you were feasting your friends on your birthday. For the poison so affected the bodies and minds of those present that you all talked at once, and sang absurd songs, and when you got up to dance, not

M

only did not keep time, but could not even stand upright.'
And Astyages said, 'Does not your father drink wine,
boy?' 'Certainly he drinks it,' answered Cyrus, 'but he
suffers nothing of that kind, for Sacas does not pour it
out for him.'

287. On the 19th of April the Albanians revolted from
the Turks. They held a meeting at Scodra to declare
themselves independent, and their leader spoke as follows: 'Brethren, when they sold us to our enemies, that
mountain race, which is of all nations the most barbarous,
they did not know who we were, or what institutions
we enjoyed. We, the descendants of Alexander the
Great, surrounded by wolves eager for prey, shall know
how to defend the tombs of our fathers. To-morrow our
brethren will be delivered over to the enemy. Will you
allow this?' The whole assembly answered that they
would not. He then said that for fifty years he had
served the Sultan, but now he separated himself from
him, and recognised no longer any lord. Then having
torn off the medals from his breast, he dashed them on
the ground, and bade them show themselves worthy of
this enterprise, and first tear down the crescent banner,
and set up the Albanian flag in its place. When this
was done he said that they had arms already, and could
find hands to wield them; nothing but money was wanting to the Albanians, who were brave but poor.

288. A thousand foot soldiers were put at the disposal
of Alexis, together with a picked company of thirty horsemen. These had secret orders given them to obey their
leader implicitly in every particular. Whatever enterprise

Alexis might call upon them to engage in, however sudden, however unexpected, however rash it seemed, they were to carry out his orders without question asked; and to look upon that enterprise as the sole object of the campaign. When the day for action came, Alexis, after parting with the king, whom he had accompanied in his ride around the camp, called his troopers together, and said, 'We have now, my men, to brace ourselves up to do the deed which you were commanded to execute under my guidance.'

289. 'Be ready heart and hand; and let no one hesitate to do as he sees me doing. The man who hangs back, or tries to cross my purpose, I tell him, he shall never see his home again.' A shudder ran through them all, as they remembered their secret orders. By this time the king was seen approaching. Alexis ordered them to couch their spears, and 'keep your eyes on me,' he said. Pausing a moment to collect himself before taking the irrevocable step, he charged the tyrant as he approached, transfixed his horse, and dashed the rider to the ground; where the troopers despatched him as he lay.

290. The Indians rushed on, a host against a man; as having nothing to do but to despatch the prey that had fallen into their hands. But Alexander, who was now partly sheltered by the wall, and also by the trunk and spreading boughs of an old tree that grew near it, kept his assailants at bay with his wonted vigour. Their chief and another, who ventured within reach of his sword, paid for their rashness with their lives. Two more, before they came quite so near, he disabled, after the manner of a Homeric combat, with stones. The rest, deterred by these examples, kept at a safe distance, and only plied him with missiles, which were mostly intercepted by the branches under which he stood, leaning either against the trunk or the wall.

Livy.

291. On the second day his voyage was interrupted by a gale which, meeting the rapid current of the Indus, caused a swell, in which the galleys became unmanageable. Most of them were severely damaged, many went to pieces, either afloat or after they had been run aground. While the shipwrights were repairing the disaster, Alexander sent a few light troops up the country, in search of natives who might serve as pilots. A few were taken, well acquainted with the navigation of the river; and under their guidance he continued his voyage to the sea. Near the mouth it still blew so hard from the sea that he was fain to take shelter in a canal pointed out by the Indians. And here the Macedonians were first astonished by the ebb of the tide, when they saw their vessels suddenly stranded.

Livy, xxviii. 30.

292. Although there is nothing new to tell you, and I am rather expecting a letter from you, or better still your arrival in person; yet, as the messenger was starting I could not let him go without sending you a line. Mind you come as soon as you can. We are all eagerly expecting you, be assured of that. Not only ourselves, the family, I mean, but everybody. I was half inclined to fear that you would put off your visit. But seeing how important it is in your own interests that you should come as soon as possible, I have ventured to give you this reminder. I have already told you what my wishes are : for the rest you must use your own judgment. And please let me know when we may expect you. Good bye.

Rome, Feb. 11th.

293. The enterprise was attended with more difficulty than was expected. The infidels had ploughed up the lands in the neighbourhood ; and as the light cavalry of the Spaniards was working its way through the deep furrows, the Moors opened the canals which intersected the fields, and in a moment the horses were floundering up to their girths in the mire and water. Thus embarrassed in their progress, the Spaniards presented a fatal mark to the Moorish missiles, which rained on them with pitiless fury ; and it was not without great efforts and considerable loss that they gained a firm landing on the opposite side. Undismayed however they then charged the enemy with such vivacity as compelled him to give way and take refuge within the fortifications of the town.

294. No impediment could now check the ardour of the assailants. They threw themselves from their horses, and bringing forward the scaling-ladders, planted them against the walls. Gonsalvo was the first to gain the summit ; and as a powerful Moor endeavoured to thrust him from the topmost round of the ladder, he grasped the battlements firmly with his left hand, and dealt the infidel such a blow with the sword in his right as brought him headlong to the ground. He then leapt into the place, and was speedily followed by his troops. The enemy made but a brief and ineffectual resistance. The greater part were put to the sword : the remainder, including the women and children, were made slaves, and the town was delivered up to pillage.

295. It was determined by the chiefs to strike at once into the heart of the Red Sierra, as it was called from the colour of its rocks, rising to the east of Ronda, and the principal theatre of insurrection. On the 18th of March the army encamped before Monarda, on the skirts of a mountain, where the Moors were understood to have assembled in considerable force. They had not been long in these quarters before parties of the enemy were seen hovering along the slopes of the mountain, from which the Christian camp was divided by a narrow river. Aguilar's troops, who occupied the van, were so much roused by the sight of the enemy, that a small party, seizing a banner, rushed across the stream without orders, in pursuit of them. The odds however were so great that they would have been severely handled, had not Aguilar, while he bitterly condemned their temerity, advanced to their support with the rest of his corps.

296. It has been the custom for the prosecutor in cases of treason like the present, to dwell on the heinous-ness of the crime : to describe the disastrous effects that would have followed on success ; the subversion of order; the triumph of anarchy; the reign of terror, with revenge, murder, rapine and all their attendant miseries. But if the object is to inflame your anger against the prisoners, surely there is no need. The facts speak for themselves, and it is but rhetoric thrown away. But, my lords, in the present instance vindictiveness would be a blunder. It is not through indifference to the enormity of their crime that I say this, no man underrates the injuries directed against himself. But the licence of retaliation is different in different cases.

297. Men of low degree who pass their lives in obscurity may be angry and sin, for few will be the wiser. The sphere of their fame is as limited as their fortune. But rank has corresponding obligations. When men are set in high places all the world knows of their doings. The more exalted the position the more limited the charter. Princes cannot do as they like. They may not indulge in likes and dislikes; least of all may they give way to temper. What in other men is mere caprice, is called tyranny and oppression in the occupant of a throne. I admit that no punishment could be great enough for the guilt of these men. But last impressions are always the most vivid, and in the case of criminals people forget the crime, but cease not to talk about the punishment, if it happens to be of more than ordinary severity.

298. 'And yet,' I continued, 'we have not discussed the principal wages of virtue, and the greatest of the prizes that are held out to it.'

'If there are others greater than those already mentioned, they must be of extraordinary magnitude.'

'But how,' I replied, 'can anything great be compressed into a brief space of time? And the whole interval between childhood and old age is brief, I conceive, compared to eternity.'

'Rather describe it as nothing.'

'What then?   Do you think that it is the duty of an immortal thing to trouble itself about this insignificant interval, and not about eternity?'

'I think it ought to concern itself about eternity: but what do you mean by this?'

'Have you not learned,' I asked, 'that our soul is immortal, and never dies?'

He looked at me, and said in amazement, 'No, really - -I have not; but can you maintain this doctrine?'

'Yes, as I am an honest man,' I replied; 'and I think you could also.   It is quite easy to do it.'

'Not to me,' he said; 'at the same time I should be glad to hear from you what, by your account, is so easy.'

Cicero, *Tusc. Quæst.* i. 5, § 9.

299. The fate of Valens himself was never exactly known.   Some said that at nightfall he fell mortally wounded by an arrow, and that his body, confounded among those of the common soldiers, could never be recognised.   Others asserted, that when he was wounded, some of his guards conveyed him to a neighbouring cottage, and while they were engaged in trying to dress his wound, the enemy surrounded the house, and being unable to force the doors, heaped straw and wood against them, and setting fire to these materials, burned the house and all within it.   One of the guards who escaped out of a window survived to tell the story.

Such was the end of the Emperor Valens, in the fiftieth year of his age, and the fourteenth of his reign. He is said to have been a firm friend, a rigid maintainer of both civil and military order, a mild ruler of the provinces. On the other hand, he is charged with avarice, indolence, severity bordering on cruelty; and it is added, that though affecting a great regard for justice, he would never allow the judges to give any sentence but such as he wished.

Livy, i. 16.

Tacitus, *Hist.* ii. 49, 72.

300. It was evening when the ambassadors arrived at the Roman camp. Carus was at that time seated on the grass eating his supper, which consisted of a bowl of cold boiled peas, and some pieces of salt pork, with a purple woollen robe thrown over his shoulders. He desired them to be brought to him, and when they came he told them that if their master did not submit he would in a month's time make Persia as bare of trees and standing corn as his own head was of hair ; and, suiting the action to the word, he pulled off the cap he wore, and displayed his head totally devoid of hair. He invited them, if they were hungry, to share his meal; if not, he bade them depart. They withdrew in terror. Carus forthwith took the field, and recovered the whole of Mesopotamia. He defeated the troops sent against him, and took the cities of Seleucia and Ctesiphon.

Livy, iii. 26.

THE END.

Now ready, small quarto, pp. xii, 1192, bevelled boards, red edges, price Eighteen Shillings.

A LATIN DICTIONARY

FOR

SCHOOLS

BY

CHARLTON T. LEWIS, Ph.D.

EDITOR OF 'LEWIS AND SHORT'S LATIN DICTIONARY.'

Also, by CHARLTON T. LEWIS, PH.D., *in conjunction with* CHARLES SHORT, LL.D., *Professor of Latin in Columbia College, New York.*

Quarto, pp. xiv, 2020, cloth, price Twenty-Five Shillings.

A LATIN DICTIONARY

FOUNDED ON ANDREWS' EDITION OF FREUND'S LATIN DICTIONARY

REVISED, ENLARGED, AND IN GREAT PART REWRITTEN.

'Must supersede all its rivals for common use.'—*Prof. J. E. B. Mayor in 'Notes and Queries.'*

'The work of Messrs. Lewis and Short is a real advance on any previous Latin-English Dictionary. The orthography has been corrected throughout, a step which, however obvious, easy, and necessary, is of immense practical benefit to Latin scholarship in England, where we have for some time, in books available for school teaching, been troubled with mere confusion in this matter.'—*Professor Nettleship in the 'Academy.'*

Oxford

AT THE CLARENDON PRESS

LONDON: HENRY FROWDE

OXFORD UNIVERSITY PRESS WAREHOUSE, AMEN CORNER, E.C.

By HENRY NETTLESHIP, M.A., Corpus Professor of Latin.

THE ROMAN SATURA : *its original form in connection with its literary development.* 8vo. sewed, 1s.

ANCIENT LIVES OF VERGIL; *with an Essay on the Poems of Vergil.* 8vo. sewed, 2s.

LECTURES AND ESSAYS ON SUBJECTS CONNECTED WITH LATIN LITERATURE AND SCHOLARSHIP. *Crown 8vo. 7s. 6d.*

By W. Y. SELLAR, M.A., Professor of Humanity, Edinburgh.

THE ROMAN POETS OF THE AUGUSTAN AGE. VIRGIL. *Second Edition. Crown 8vo.* cloth, 9s.

THE ROMAN POETS OF THE REPUBLIC. *New Edition, Revised and Enlarged.* 8vo. cloth, 14s.

By JOHN WORDSWORTH, D.D., Bishop of Salisbury.

FRAGMENTS AND SPECIMENS OF EARLY LATIN. *With Introduction and Notes.* 8vo. cloth, 18s.

By NORTH PINDER, M.A.

SELECTIONS FROM THE LESS KNOWN LATIN POETS. *Demy 8vo.* cloth, 15s.

EDITED BY THE REV. T. L. PAPILLON, M.A.

P. VERGILI MARONIS OPERA. *With Introduction and Notes. Vol. I. Introduction and Text. Vol. II. Notes. Crown 8vo.* 10s. 6d.

Vol. I. separately, 4s. 6d.

OXFORD: AT THE CLARENDON PRESS

LONDON: HENRY FROWDE

OXFORD UNIVERSITY PRESS WAREHOUSE, AMEN CORNER, E.C.

Clarendon Press Series.

Latin School-books.

[A]

Sargent. *Easy Passages for Translation into Latin.* By J. Y. SARGENT, M.A. *Seventh Edition.* . . . . . . [Extra fcap. 8vo. 2s. 6d.

[*A Key to this Edition is provided : for Teachers only, price 5s.*]

—— *A Latin Prose Primer.* By the same Author.

[Extra fcap. 8vo. 2s. 6d.

King and **Cookson.** The Principles of Sound and Inflexion, as illustrated in the Greek and Latin Languages. By J. E. KING, M.A., and CHRISTOPHER COOKSON, M.A. [8vo. 18s.

Papillon. *A Manual of Comparative Philology.* By T. L. PAPILLON, M.A. *Third Edition.* [Crown 8vo. 6s.

LATIN CLASSICS FOR SCHOOLS.

Caesar. *The Commentaries* (for Schools). With Notes and Maps. BY CHARLES E. MOBERLY, M.A.

The Gallic War. Second Edition.	[Extra fcap. 8vo. 4s. 6d.
The Gallic War. Books I, II. .	. [Extra fcap. 8vo. 2s.
The Gallic War. Books III–V. .	. . [In the Press.
The Civil War. Second Edition.	[Extra fcap. 8vo. 3s. 6d.
The Civil War. Book I. . .	. [Extra fcap. 8vo. 2s.

Catulli Veronensis *Carmina Selecta,* secundum recognitionem ROBINSON ELLIS, A.M. . . . . . . [Extra fcap. 8vo. 3s. 6d.

Cicero. *Selection of Interesting and Descriptive Passages.* With Notes. By HENRY WALFORD, M.A. In three Parts. *Third Edition.* ·

[Extra fcap. 8vo. 4s. 6d.

Part I. *Anecdotes from Grecian and Roman History.* . [*limp*, 1s. 6d.
Part II. *Omens and Dreams; Beauties of Nature.* . . [„ 1s. 6d.
Part III. *Rome's Rule of her Provinces.* . . . . [„ 1s. 6d.

—— *De Senectute.* With Introduction and Notes. By LEONARD HUXLEY, B.A. *In one or two Parts.* . . . . [Extra fcap. 8vo. 2s.

—— *Pro Cluentio.* With Introduction and Notes. By W. RAMSAY, M.A. Edited by G. G. RAMSAY, M.A. *Second Edition.* [Extra fcap. 8vo. 3s. 6d.

—— *Select Orations* (for Schools). *In Verrem Actio Prima. De Imperio Gn. Pompeii. Pro Archia. Philippica IX.* With Introduction and Notes. By J. R. KING, M.A. *Second Edition.* . [Extra fcap. 8vo. 2s. 6d.

—— *In Q. Caecilium Divinatio* and *In C. Verrem Actio Prima.* With Introduction and Notes. By J. R. KING, M.A. [Extra fcap. 8vo., 1s. 6d.

—— *Speeches against Catilina.* With Introduction and Notes. By E. A. UPCOTT M.A. *In one or two Parts.* . . [Extra fcap. 8vo. 2s. 6d.

—— *Philippic Orations.* With Notes, etc., by J. R. KING, M.A. *Second Edition.* . . . . [8vo. 10s. 6d.

Cicero. *Selected Letters* (for Schools). With Notes. By C. E.
PRICHARD, M.A., and E. R. BERNARD, M.A. *Second Edition.*
[Extra fcap. 8vo. 3*s.*

—— *Select Letters.* With English Introductions, Notes, and Ap-
pendices. By ALBERT WATSON, M.A. *Third Edition.* . . [8vo. 18*s.*

—— *Select Letters.* Text. By the same Editor. *Second Edition.*
[Extra fcap. 8vo. 4*s.*

Cornelius Nepos. With Notes. By OSCAR BROWNING, M.A.
Third Edition. Revised by W. R. INGE, M.A. . . [Extra fcap. 8vo. 3*s.*

Horace. With a Commentary. Volume I. *The Odes, Carmen.*
Seculare, and *Epodes.* By EDWARD C. WICKHAM, M.A., Head Master of
Wellington College. *New Edition. In one or two Parts.* [Extra fcap. 8vo. 6*s.*

—— *Selected Odes.* With Notes for the use of a Fifth Form. By
E. C. WICKHAM, M.A. *In one or two Parts.* . . . [Extra fcap. 8vo. 2*s.*

Juvenal. *XIII Satires.* Edited, with Introduction, Notes, etc., by
C. H. PEARSON, M.A., and H. A. STRONG, M.A. . . [Crown 8vo. 6*s.*
Or separately, Text and Introduction, 3s. ; Notes, 3s. 6d.

Livy. *Selections* (for Schools). With Notes and Maps. By H. LEE-
WARNER, M.A. . . . . [Extra fcap. 8vo.

Part I. *The Caudine Disaster.* . . . . . . [*limp,* 1*s.* 6*d.*
Part II. *Hannibal's Campaign in Italy.* . . . . [,, 1*s.* 6*d.*
Part III. *The Macedonian War.* . . . . . . [,, 1*s.* 6*d.*

—— *Book I.* With Introduction, Historical Examination, and Notes.
By J. R. SEELEY, M.A. *Second Edition.* . . . . . . [8vo. 6*s.*

—— *Books V—VII.* With Introduction and Notes. By A. R. CLUER,
B.A. *Second Edition.* Revised by P. E. MATHESON, M.A. *In one or two
Parts.* . . . . [Extra fcap. 8vo. 5*s.*

—— *Book V.* By the same Editors. . . . [*In the Press.*

—— *Books XXI—XXIII.* With Introduction, Notes and Maps.
By M. T. TATHAM, M.A. *Second Edition. In one or two Parts.*
[Extra fcap. 8vo. 5*s.*

—— *Book XXI.* By the same Editor. . . . [*In the Press.*

—— *Book XXII.* With Introduction, Notes and Maps. By the
same Editor. . . . . . . [Extra fcap. 8vo. 2*s.* 6*d.*

Ovid. *Selections* (for the use of Schools). With Introductions and
Notes, and an Appendix on the Roman Calendar. By W. RAMSAY, M.A.
Edited by G. G. RAMSAY, M.A. *Third Edition.* . [Extra fcap. 8vo. 5*s.* 6*d.*

—— *Tristia,* Book I. The Text revised, with an Introduction and
Notes. By S. G. OWEN, B.A. . . . . [Extra fcap. 8vo. 3*s.* 6*d.*

Persius. *The Satires.* With Translation and Commentary by
J. CONINGTON, M.A., edited by H. NETTLESHIP, M.A. *Second Edition.*
[8vo. 7*s.* 6*d.*

Plautus. *Captivi.* With Introduction and Notes. By W. M. LINDSAY, M.A. *In one or two Parts.* . . . . . [Extra fcap. 8vo. 2s. 6d.

—— *Trinummus.* With Notes and Introductions. (Intended. for the Higher Forms of Public Schools.) By C. E. FREEMAN, M.A., and A. SLOMAN, M.A. . . . . [Extra fcap. 8vo. 3s.

Pliny. *Selected Letters* (for Schools). With Notes. By C. E. PRICHARD, M.A., and E. R. BERNARD, M.A. *New Edition. In one or two Parts.* . . . . [Extra fcap. 8vo. 3s.

Sallust. *Bellum Catilinarium* and *Jugurthinum.* With Introduction and Notes, by W. W. CAPES, M.A. . . [Extra fcap. 8vo. 4s. 6d.

Tacitus. *The Annals.* Books I—IV. Edited, with Introduction and Notes for the use of Schools and Junior Students, by H. FURNEAUX, M A. . [Extra fcap. 8vo. 5s.

—— *The Annals.* Book I. By the same Editor.
[Extra fcap. 8vo. *limp*, 2s.

Terence. *Adelphi.* With Notes and Introductions. By A. SLOMAN, M.A. . . . . [Extra fcap. 8vo. 3s.

—— *Andria.* With Notes and Introductions. By C. E. FREEMAN, M.A., and A. SLOMAN, M.A. . . . . . . [Extra fcap. 8vo. 3s.

—— *Phormio.* With Notes and Introductions. By A. SLOMAN, M.A. . . . . [Extra fcap. 8vo. 3s.

Tibullus and **Propertius.** *Selections.* Edited, with Introduction and Notes, by G. G. RAMSAY, M.A. *In one or two Parts.* [Extra fcap. 8vo. 6s.

Virgil. With Introduction and Notes, by T. L. PAPILLON, M.A. In Two Volumes. . . . [Crown 8vo. 10s. 6d.; Text separately, 4s. 6d.

—— *Bucolics.* With Introduction and Notes, by C. S. JERRAM, M.A. *In one or two Parts.* [Extra fcap. 8vo. 2s. 6d.

—— *Georgics.* By the same Editor. . . . [*In the Press.*

—— *Aeneid I.* With Introduction and Notes, by the same Editor.
[Extra fcap. 8vo. *limp*, 1s. 6d.

—— *Aeneid IX.* Edited with Introduction and Notes, by A. E. HAIGH, M.A. . . . [Extra fcap. 8vo. *limp*, 1s. 6d. *In two Parts*, 2s.

London: HENRY FROWDE,

OXFORD UNIVERSITY PRESS WAREHOUSE, AMEN CORNER.

Edinburgh: 6 QUEEN STREET.

Oxford: CLARENDON PRESS DEPOSITORY,
116 HIGH STREET.

A Reading Room has been opened at the Clarendon Press Warehouse, Amen Corner, for the use of members of the University of Oxford. Schoolmasters and others, not being members, can also use it on obtaining permission. .